MURPHY'S CINDERELLA

BECKE TURNER

Special-T Publishing

SUNBERRY, NORTH CAROLINA

A place to call home.

Welcome to fictitious Sunberry, North Carolina. Settle back, put your feet up and prepare to enjoy a basketful of southern hospitality. With a population of twenty thousand diverse residents, Sunberry is the small city Americans dream of calling home. This slice of southern comfort offers a four-year college, an historic opera house complete with second-level entertainment, and a full-service hospital. No need to feel like a stranger. Sunberry residents mingle with new inhabitants, especially service members returning to civilian life.

If you're a veteran from nearby Camp Lejeune, a local rancher breeding organic cattle along the river, or a dog trainer developing new puppies to assist the disabled, you're bound to find a happily ever after in Sunberry. After all, doesn't everyone crave a home?

CHAPTER ONE

D r. Kyle Murphy tugged at the collar of his stiff tuxedo shirt and wiggled his cramped toes. The shiny rental shoes rubbed his heels worse than the three-hundred-dollar tux rubbed his bank account. But he couldn't blow off the event—not when his colleagues had awarded him Physician of the Quarter. Now if only Triangle Oncology would offer him a partnership.

"Congratulations." A young man, who looked younger than his little brother Nate, nodded.

Kyle raised his hand but didn't hasten his pace. Based on the fire in his right heel, a three-centimeter blister had surfaced. That burn, however, was nothing compared to the one box he hadn't checked. In twelve more emergency department shifts, he'd write the check and remove the monkey from his back. But first, he had to get the partnership.

Trying not to limp, he checked his phone. No texts from 6-West, the oncology unit where he admitted his patients. He needed to check alternate treatment options for Mrs. Brown. There had to be something to slow her disease progression.

You can't save everyone. His mother's voice whispered in his mind. Mom didn't get it. His work couldn't make up for his past mistakes. Nothing could do that. But every time one of his patients went into remission, a family got more time— time to raise a child, time to love a family member, time to live.

Ahead in the hotel ballroom, the lights dimmed. The hum of voices and laughter lowered a level. He halted and a grunt of horror leaked from his throat. Guarding the entrance to the darkened room, the full-length, life-size photo of his image mocked him.

So much for an 8x10 black and white on the hospital's Wall of Shame, as the docs referred to the hallway leading to the lobby with the latest honorees. No one had mentioned the 6-foot drop-down screen with his unsmiling mug on it. Good thing he hadn't let the photographer talk him into removing his glasses.

"Dr. Murphy?" The door attendant handed him a program. The young woman couldn't be older than his little sister, Hope. "The ceremony's starting. I need to close the doors."

Kyle extracted his phone from his pocket. "Go ahead. I've got to take this call. I'll be there in a few minutes."

Could he get away with ditching the awards banquet to make rounds at the hospital? A white lie to the awards committee that he'd received a last-minute call from a patient might work. Besides, he was known for his evening rounds when the floor quieted.

When a muffled laugh filtered through the hallway, he turned and froze. At the other ballroom entrance, a matching banner of Nurse Dana Graham, who was also receiving an award, guarded the door.

Unlike his photo, the photographer had captured her generous spirit. The poster reminded him of his brother's

NFL team photo in a way. Instead of a professional wide receiver, Whit resembled a T-ball coach. Whit and Dana possessed an inner light people noticed. Some people were special like that. Never asking anything for themselves, but always willing to go the extra mile for someone else.

An ache gnawed at his belly. He pulled open the heavy ballroom door. If he positioned right, Triangle Oncology might offer him a partnership. Once he had an offer, he'd consider a family of his own. He stepped inside the darkened room and shut out the lonely voice that whispered he'd never be able to replace the family he betrayed.

Using the stage lighting as a guide, Kyle moved through the tables decorated with silver streamers and blue balloons, nodding at key hospital associates, including the Triangle partners. He halted on the red carpet when he located his tribe seated at the three tables designated to the 6-West oncology unit. Only one vacant chair remained—beside Dana Graham. The power bar he chowed down on the way to the hotel churned in his gut. What were the stinking chances out of twenty-four flipping chairs he'd get the one beside Dana?

He turned the vacant chair to face the stage, aligning with Dana and the unit manager, Paula.

Something cold and wet covered his hand.

"Oops!" Dana set down her drink and grabbed a napkin. "So sorry."

His heart rate tripled, drumming against his ribs. "Good evening, Nurse Ratchet."

Dana slanted him a look, and he could swear her lip twitched. "Sit down, Dr. Frankenstein. I don't want to miss the stunning conclusion of Wilcox Memorial's annual statistics."

"I can't help it." He dropped onto the padded chair. "I was always the kid who talked in class, especially the boring ones."

And he'd better start talking fast because dressed in her evening clothes Nurse Ratchet looked more like Nurse Fantasy. Besides, if he didn't run his mouth, some other part of his anatomy might take off.

"Well, I was the kid who followed the rules," she stage-whispered.

"I'm shocked," he lied.

"We broke even last year." Paula raised her voice to be heard over the clapping audience.

"Darn." Kyle pressed his hands over his heart. "I hate when that happens."

"It beats walking up on stage." Even with the dying applause, Dana's bite of sarcasm faded into something...different.

"Are you okay?"

She shook her head, and a wisp of brown hair tempted him to rub it between his thumb and index finger. No doubt, it would be silky—

He straightened in his chair and curled his hand into a fist. "What can I do to help?"

She blew out a tortured breath, and the wisp of hair danced in front of her face. "Read my essay."

"Your colleagues want to hear from you," Paula whispered.

"Mom and Robin attracted the spotlight in my family. I'm a cheer-from-the-sidelines kind of girl."

With her curvy body, rosy complexion, and high energy, Dana embodied health. But a sickly pallor had replaced her healthy glow. When his patients turned that color, he ordered antiemetics.

"Your essay will touch everyone in this room," Paula said.

"If your family doesn't cheer loud enough for you, I'll whistle with my fingers." He gave her his best grin. "It's guaranteed to pierce an eardrum or two."

"Thanks. But right now, I just want to slowly sink beneath the table." Dana sipped her water. "I can't do this."

He straightened. Nurse Ratchet couldn't do something? Surprise, surprise. He'd dubbed her Nurse Ratchet because of her fierce patient advocacy, usually opposing him.

"After going toe-to-toe with me for the past six months, you should be able to do anything." Except she looked terrified. "You're the most courageous person I know."

"When I'm arguing informed decision with you, I'm not standing on three-inch heels and navigating stairs in a tight gown."

Good thing. On the floor, cancer treatment demanded his focus, something at risk with her bare shoulder and impressive curves within touching distance.

"I've been coveting those silver sandals all night," Paula whispered.

"Great! You can have them." Dana leaned to the side. "I swear my little toes are hamburger. I'll probably leave a blood trail to the stage."

Yeah, he could relate. "I could escort you to the podium."

Dana squeezed his forearm. "Would you?" She turned to Paula. "It could work. No one would know it's not part of the plan."

"No one but the planning committee." Paula shrugged. "It's not like they would stop him."

"And you'd wait until I'm done and help me down the stairs?" Dana said.

Was she kidding? When she looked at him with those big blue eyes, he'd probably sit up and beg. Ah, no. He wouldn't go that far. A man had to reserve a little pride.

"Sure."

"Don't let me fall." She canted her chin to the right. "I swear if I breathe wrong, I'm going to pop a seam."

"That dress is to die for," Paula said.

He'd second her opinion.

"Well, the underwear holding me in it may kill me."

Paula grinned. "No wonder you passed on dessert."

"TMI," Kyle said. They acted like he was deaf—and a eunuch. Imagining Dana in her underwear was *not* a good visual, especially if he planned to escort her on stage.

"Really, *Doctor*." Dana's brows lifted just like Mom's when his sister did the drama-queen act. "Professional healthcare staff are equal-opportunity humiliators. There are no taboo topics in medicine."

When he saluted her, she fashioned one big blue into the stink eye. Man, she was cute. And he'd lost his mind. He raised his hand in surrender. If he'd possessed a functioning brain cell, he would've added a white linen napkin. Good thing the emcee saved his sorry butt with Dana's introduction. The crowd erupted into applause, and her complexion returned to a sickly gray.

Although the urge to tuck her beside him curled his hands, he stood and held out his forearm. Her hand trembled on his sleeve, and he covered her long fingers with his. When he squeezed, she bit her bottom lip. He'd give his right arm to take her away from all of this, but she deserved to be honored for her work and her big heart. He sucked in a breath. What would it be like to have her big heart care for him?

"I've got you, beautiful." Heat fired his neck, his cheeks, and his ears. Where the heck did that come from? He didn't talk to women like that. He didn't even think like that. He was relieved she didn't respond to his lame comment.

While the crowd stood, their applause deafening the room, Kyle escorted her up the three metal stairs to the podium. Panic widened her eyes, but she kept her back ramrod straight and faced the crowd. His jacket tugged across his chest. It wasn't like she was with him. Heck, he didn't think she even liked him. Still, he was proud to deliver her to the podium to accept her award, proud to know and work with her, and even prouder when she started speaking.

"My patients remind me every day of how precious my life is," Dana started. "If you view these realizations as gifts, your life is one celebration after another. Do you know what an honor it is to share the final moments of a person's life? People often ask if my work is depressing? Every day, I learn something new about this precious thing we know as life. I don't focus on life's end. I look for ways to enrich my life and the lives of the people I touch. When I succeed, I make a difference to another's life."

She paused and Kyle, waiting at the side of the stage, could swear no one in the room breathed. He sure hadn't.

"There are many opportunities to give of yourself to another," she continued. "Some people say to stop and smell the flowers. I say, stop and acknowledge the gift of giving. How can I help? How can I learn? How can I share? In the last days of life, people often make incredible discoveries. It's an honor when they share those insights with me. I become a link in humanity. I honor their gift by listening and learning to lead a fuller life. That's the gift of giving. Every time I succeed, it brightens my day, teaches me something new about myself, makes me better for the next person I touch."

Kyle swallowed past the tightness in his throat. He got it. When one of his patients went into remission, he felt good because his work had given them more time, but honored? Interesting perspective, which figured. Dana was an interesting woman.

When she closed twenty minutes later, sniffling filtered through the audience. Even his eyes were stinging, and he never cried. His patients didn't need tears. They needed his intellect. They needed treatment options.

The crowd stood, and he stepped into the glare of the stage lights. The stupid things nearly blinded him. For an instant, Dana's outline darkened the glare. He blinked, and her features focused. Tears moistened her eyes. She grabbed his wrist when he reached toward her.

Once they navigated down the stairs, he could've let her go. He didn't. His hand was numb from her grip, but he didn't care. If he could steady her—even for a moment—he'd do it. Her words circled in his head, and a cheesy grin stretched his face. He was honored to escort her to their table.

She nodded and thanked the colleagues who congratulated her, weeping the whole time. The tears didn't seem to embarrass her. Note to self: carry a handkerchief like his stepdad Ryan did for Mom.

At the table, he stepped back and reluctantly released her. Paula stood and hugged her the way he'd wanted to do the moment her perfume tickled his nostrils. The scent was probably stronger along the column of her neck. The curve of her jaw lured him like a kid to a sugar cookie.

"Congratulations." Kyle checked his wristwatch to busy his empty hands. "You deserve the honor."

Although a few questions about her patient-care perspective loomed in his mind, he shook them off, which annoyed him. Nothing worse than yearning for an answer when you couldn't satisfy the need. He'd research it tonight. Dana couldn't be the only one with that perspective. In the meantime, he needed to maneuver toward Triangle's table. It never hurt to let them know he was still around, still interested in a partnership. He'd read a white paper on a new myeloma treatment. If he engaged them in a conversation, he could demonstrate he was on top of his game.

Within fifteen minutes, he'd made a quick acceptance speech for his award, and the emcee had closed the ceremony for dancing and cocktails. Cocktails won for the hospital staff.

While a sparkling ball dropped above the small portable

dance floor, the hotel staff disassembled the stage, and a DJ started a song Kyle didn't recognize. Big surprise. He'd been humping to get through med school the last six years. His favorite tunes played on the oldie stations now.

A nurse from the second shift squealed and stood. "I love this song!"

Within seconds, the three tables emptied, leaving him alone with Dana.

"Don't you dance?" a male voice said from behind him.

Kyle turned to greet Triangle's junior partner, Greg Johnson, standing with a stunning blond Kyle guessed to be his wife. Kyle scanned the empty tables and slammed into Dana's amused expression.

He swallowed a complaint. It could've been karaoke. Hope taught him to limit his sing-alongs to the shower because he couldn't carry a tune in a bucket. But if Triangle partners wanted associates who practiced good medicine *and* danced, he'd be their man.

He pushed to his feet. "I can make a fool of myself the same as the next guy."

Greg's wife tugged at her husband's hand, and he shot Kyle a beseeching look. "Thank goodness. Misery loves company."

Got that right. Kyle turned to Dana. With her lips pressed into a thin line, she didn't encourage a man. But, hey, he needed a Triangle partnership.

"Cut me some slack," he whispered. "I got you safely up and down the stage stairs."

She tugged at the top of her gown. "Duly noted. But after this dance, we're going to discuss transparency in medicine."

He should've seen that coming. There was always a price, and Dana never avoided a discussion about medical ethics. For now, he just had to keep her perfume from going to his head.

"Agreed." The admission passed through his larynx like a razor blade. "Now, *please* dance with me."

If he laughed at her stink eye, she'd probably clobber him. "Since when do you agree with me?"

Dana would be the one to poke a sleeping bear if it meant she'd move her position forward. But he needed to get on the dance floor and show the partners he was part of the Wilcox Memorial community.

"You're the belle of the ball, and you look beautiful." He held out his hand to her. "You've obviously gone to a lot of effort to create that look. Let me show you off on the dance floor for your Cinderella moment."

Inside, he cringed. But that's what Mom had called it. The hokey words made him sound like a fool. Although it had been a long time since he'd taken a girl to the prom, he'd learned to trust Mom's girl advice. Except Dana was no girl. She was a woman with a strong sense of right and wrong—according to Dana Graham.

A bead of sweat tickled his forehead, and his glasses slid down his nose. He swallowed. *Come on, Dana. You're killing me here.*

He motioned her forward. "I promise not to step on your toes."

Although she gave him a look like they were headed to a firing squad, she stood and took his hand. Her roughened fingers from constant handwashing rasped his. Dana was no pampered babe. She worked hard, just like he did. Good to know they had a few common traits. He hesitated, and she bumped against him.

"And I'm holding you to your promise to avoid my toes," she said. "They've suffered enough abuse sporting these shoes."

He turned to her. "Got it. If it's any comfort, my rental shoes have rubbed a blister on my heel."

Her brows raised an inch up her forehead. "I'll take off mine if you'll take off yours."

What? His brain seized along with every other working element in his body.

She squinted at him. "Hello?"

His lips moved, which was amazing because he could've sworn they were glued to his teeth. He needed a drink.

The song ended, and the DJ replaced it with the mournful strains of a ballad. Kyle glanced at the stupid disco ball and breathed past the constriction in his chest. A slow dance, no less? Terrific. Why didn't the DJ open his jugular? Better yet, why couldn't he think about something other than what was beneath her dress?

Dana snapped her fingers an inch from his nose. "Hey, Prince Charming. I thought you wanted to dance."

Then she slid her arms around his neck and pulled him close, so her perfume infused his already foggy brain, and her soft curves scorched his chest. Worse, his heart stuttered like he'd missed an important patient symptom.

Quit thinking about her body and focus on this morning.

With his hands resting slightly above her hips, they swayed to the music. Her thigh brushed against his. Satiny flesh rubbed his chin. Her fingers stroked the hairs at the back of his neck.

He needed a haircut. He needed her closer. Cinnamon? She smelled like Grandma Stella's kitchen on Thanksgiving. His eyes drifted closed. He snapped them open and focused on the words to the song.

"Are they playing this for you?" Man, she smelled good.

She pulled back to meet his gaze. "I'm sorry. I didn't hear the question."

He stumbled, barely missing her toes, but her voice? Since when was it kind of smoky?

"Kyle? What was the question?"

She was gorgeous in the glittery light of the ball. The lyrics echoed in his head. The question! "They're playing a Cinderella song. I thought it might be for you."

Her gaze sharpened. "Let me guess. You aren't a country-western fan."

"I've been in class or on the floor for the past twelve years."

"They're playing Stealing Cinderella. It's about the relationship between a father and daughter."

"Well, part of the title works." And so was one portion of his brain.

She snuggled closer, and he swallowed. He didn't care what they called the tune if it would just end. This close, his foolish heart started wanting something it couldn't have. Dana was a skilled nurse and a fine woman. With her brains, looks, and sense of humor, she was the *total package*. But she wasn't for him.

The lighting emphasized the fiery highlights in her hair. At work, she brushed it back into a sassy ponytail, reminding him of a feral cat swishing its tail, ready to pounce. Tonight, she'd slicked it from her face with some sparkly thing. His glasses slid down his nose, but he didn't want to move his hands.

He should ask her out. Women always said yes to physicians. It didn't make sense, but he wasn't complaining. Male docs were still guys. Some of them were gentlemen, and some of them were jerks. She probably considered him in the jerk category, which he was. But not for the reasons she thought. He'd never been a player. He'd been a heartless SOB to his family, and Dana could verify his behavior with one meeting. She wouldn't hear it from Whit, though. No matter how bad he'd treated his little brother, Whit remained loyal. That's what made his past eat through the lining of his stomach.

Another couple bumped against them, and Dana pulled back.

"I don't know how you walk in those crazy shoes, let alone dance."

When she smiled, he could swear they turned up the lights.

"Dancing wasn't part of the plan," she whispered.

"You had a plan for the night?"

He'd hoped to get a toe in the door at Triangle Oncology. What had Dana planned?

"Dancing with you wasn't part of it." Her usual sarcasm had softened.

"That's too bad." His fingers flexed on her back, but she didn't seem to mind. "I kind of like this side of you. It's a nice change from our medical-ethics disagreements."

Her stare sharpened her features into the Dana he understood. But he didn't want to spar with her. Focusing on counting steps, he spun her to his left. It had been years since he'd slow-danced. Desperate to maintain the moment, he slid his hand to the middle of her back and pressed her into him.

She followed as he pivoted to the right. When he glanced down, her bare shoulder filled his vision. He licked his lips. She'd made patient care messy for him, but she intrigued him —on a physical level. What were the chances? He'd always appreciated a healthy woman, and Dana was all that. Besides the bare shoulder, her gauzy blue gown ran at an angle across her chest, exposing enough cleavage to make a guy wonder. The color enhanced her eyes too.

Eye color rarely drew his attention. Shoot, he'd have to think hard to come up with the eye color for his brothers. But when a woman spat and hissed like Dana in a snit, protecting her patients' rights, a guy noticed. Big, blue, and usually shooting sparks. Not tonight.

The slow song purred the final cords, and Kyle released her hand, a little surprised he didn't want to turn her loose.

"Thank you," she murmured, though her expression was far from demure.

Nope, Dana wore the same look as his little brother Nate when he did something to annoy Kyle—like hiding a dog turd in his book bag. Kyle shifted his weight to the balls of his feet, ready for an altercation, and then motioned for her to precede him. Keep a woman in clear sight so she couldn't ambush you. He knew the price at the start of the dance, but the last thing he wanted to discuss with Nurse Ratchet was medical ethics. He researched mountains of trials to secure one more day for his patients. She advocated hospice.

She wasn't changing his mind.

CHAPTER TWO

Dana snapped her slackened jaw closed and touched the back of her hand to her lips while Kyle guided her from the dance floor. Time to collect on her agreement and stop drooling over the man. But, holy cow, he'd coined the evening her Cinderella night and then made her feel like a fairy princess.

Where was Paula? This crisis called for her BFF. To her right on the dance floor, her friend's gorgeous yellow gown caught the corner of her eye. When Paula turned, she shook two thumbs up to the beat of the tune. Dana swallowed her panic and waved. With two teen boys at home, Paula deserved a night out, free from drama. Dana just hoped her head didn't explode sometime between the next minute and tomorrow at work.

Dana squared her shoulders and continued toward the table. She could do this. All she had to do was stop focusing on the warmth of Kyle's hand and start remembering his recommendation to Mrs. Brown. Her patient's chances at attaining remission were less than two percent. Two! But does he suggest hospice so she can enjoy quality time with her family? No. He recommends aggressive therapy, again.

"Thank you so much." A young woman grasped Dana's fingers between her soft brown hands. "My mother is battling breast cancer, and I felt helpless. But your words..." Tears dampened her cheeks. "Now, I'll cherish each day with her and try to be grateful for what I've been granted instead of dreading what I might lose."

"I'm glad my thoughts helped you." Dana rolled her lips. And even happier for the reminder because her thoughts about Kyle had not been positive. Why was it hard to maintain a positive outlook?

With a steadying breath, she discreetly touched her shoulder. Others might think the movement odd, but it always soothed her, reminding her of the way Mom had squeezed her shoulder and whispered encouragement despite her lack of athletic skill. Mom had believed in her. Had assured her she'd have other talents. *Can you see me now, Mom? You were right.*

Her vision clouded with tears, but her heart soared. If Mom were here, she would've sat in the front row and clapped the loudest. Everyone around her, stranger or friend, would've known her youngest daughter had been recognized. How cool was that?

"Fabulous perspective." An attractive man on her left extended his hand and snapped her attention to the present. "Chuck Benson, urology resident."

"Thanks." She glanced at Kyle. Had he increased the pressure on her back, or had she imagined it? *No more vino for you, Cinderella.*

"Do you want to move to the back of the room?" Kyle leaned close to her ear, his breath sending a shiver across her shoulders. "Our table is adjacent to the speakers, and the bass is already bouncing off my chest."

She pressed a hand above the bodice of her dress. Well, that certainly explained her heart arrhythmia. Now, for her poor tootsies. Gripping his arm, she leaned forward and unbuckled her sandals. Even in the dimmed lighting, the twin red marks highlighted her pinkies.

Kyle's forearm hardened beneath her fingers. Despite the music and the crowded room, he stood motionless above her. Confused, she glanced upward and then followed the direction of his intense gaze, which stopped on her chest.

Busted, Dr. Murphy. But it was kind of nice to get an appraising look. Still—

She yanked up her bodice, then stood and ran her arm through the sandal straps. Too bad she liked the feel of his arm beneath her hand so much. She also liked kittens, but that didn't mean she'd bring one home. The sparkly ball sent pinpoints of light frolicking across his dark hair. And then there was his tux. She swallowed past a bone-dry throat as her mind weighed the facts about Prince Charming. Aggressive treatment plans. Hot tux. Arrogant physician. Amazing physique. Oh, for goodness' sake. Straightening her spine, she strode toward the ballroom entrance and away from the pulsing woofers and tweeters.

"The lobby is quiet." He followed at her side. "Find a comfortable seat and I'll pick up another round for us."

Although he was only being nice, an arrow of annoyance slithered down her shoulders. She was the mother of an amazing five-year-old girl. Together, she and Sam created a dynamic duo. They did not need an arrogant doctor in their lives—even if she could roast a marshmallow on his smile.

To bolster her resolve, she padded from the dimmed ballroom to the bright hotel lobby. Adjacent to the registration desk, a cream sofa and side chairs welcomed weary guests. Dana sunk into the corner of the sofa and resisted the urge to plop her throbbing feet on the cocktail table. Her thoughts cleared and her heart slowed.

She stifled a yawn. Although her Cinderella night had amazed and delighted her, she needed to pull the curtain soon, especially since she'd signed up for an extra shift tomorrow. Still, her nightly cup of decaffeinated tea and cotton jammies didn't hold the usual appeal. Plus, Paula, her partner in award-night fun, remained missing with the handsome radiology technician.

Closing her eyes, Dana leaned against the overstuffed cushions. What an amazing night. When she migrated to Raleigh, she'd considered the premier hospital systems serving the North Carolina Research Triangle area, but picked Wilcox, a small hospital. Tonight, they'd picked her—and oncologist Kyle Murphy. She opened one eye. Speaking of Dr. Cutting-Edge Treatment, he was heading her way with two glasses of wine.

He handed her a glass, her final for the night. "Let's declare a moratorium on medical ethics. I've worked with you for almost eight months and know nothing about you."

It figured he'd try to wiggle out of the discussion. But she'd be leaving soon. There'd be ample time for future discussions.

She sat upright. "There's not much to tell. I'm a small-town girl from Blowing Rock, North Carolina. How about you?"

"I started out as a military brat, but Mom moved to Sunberry right after middle school." He aimed a thumb behind him. "It's on the east side of the state, about fifty miles from the ocean."

"I like the beach except for the storms."

"Says the woman from a place called Blowing Rock."

Her muscles melted into the cozy sofa corner. Wow! A sense of humor. Who knew the arrogant physician had a human side? She could learn to like this side of him. Maybe too much. So why was he still single? Wine tickled the back of her throat. Back off, girlfriend. She wasn't in the market for finding *the one*.

"Who taught you to dance?" Although it wasn't a brilliant conversation starter, it beat considering why he was easy to talk to.

His killer smile reappeared. "Mom made me practice with my brothers. She watched and critiqued our steps from the sidelines."

Dana restrained her belly laugh into a dignified chuckle. "I love an innovative woman."

A deep dimple winked at her. "Saved her toes from three clumsy teenaged boys. And yours too. I didn't even graze one."

She lifted her glass to him. "Thank you, Mrs. Murphy." What would he think if she told him she had forgotten about her mutilated feet?

He sipped his wine. "Who taught you?"

"Dad." The word came out a little funny, but the man had a way of surprising her, especially after a few glasses of wine and her giddy Cinderella night. "Mom was a Blowing Rock basketball coach, and my sister Robin was a star player. Dad and I were the cheerleaders. I guess you'd say I share a common klutz trait with your brothers. I couldn't hold onto a ball with superglue, but Dad managed to give me a few dance pointers. At least enough to get me by."

"Good thing my blister is on my heel and not my toes. I'll be sure to thank him when we meet."

Meet her Dad? Not in this lifetime. But when he stretched his long arm along the top of the sofa, almost touching her shoulder, her bum elevated from the couch cushions. Her smile might have wobbled, but she did not slide her traitorous body his way. Despite the cool room and her exposed shoulder, heat spread like a laser through her veins. With those hands, the man should've gone into vascular surgery. She swallowed. With her hormones, she should've joined an escort service. She gulped her drink.

"More wine?"

"No, thanks. I've reached my limit, and I promised Dad I'd be home before eleven."

His lashes were so long they brushed against his glasses. "You live with your parents?"

Dana coughed to hide a groan. Living with her parents sounded lame. She didn't *actually* live with her dad but the cottage in his backyard. And she was working on new living arrangements. A technicality she would eliminate in eleven overtime shifts. Besides, Kyle didn't need to know her private business.

"I moved out after college. Dad's babysitting my daughter, Samantha. Sam for short."

Big-time wrong answer! She hadn't seen such a pained expression since she'd stuck her nursing partner an inch off target with an 18-gauge needle.

"Are you okay?" she asked.

He finished his drink, then pushed his dinner jacket aside to expose the gleam of a silver wristwatch. "I have early rounds."

Disappointment straightened her spine and fired her anger. She'd almost fallen for his charm. Kyle Murphy was *the one* all right. The same kind of *one* as Sam's dad—eager for intimacy without responsibility.

He stood. "If you're ready to leave, I'll walk you to your car."

"Thanks, but Paula and I Ubered together. This is our single women's night out." She enunciated every syllable in the last sentence just to watch the man squirm. "See you on the floor."

A weird expression wrinkled his heavy brows, and his lips moved like he'd eaten spoiled food he couldn't spit out. Her breath halted, waiting for him to redeem his tacky behavior. Silence. Yep, she'd been right all along. Dr. Murphy was a gifted physician and a first-class turd.

After a beat, he nodded and exited the hotel. By the time his lanky form faded into the night's shadows, Paula's joyful laugh rang through the hallway.

"There you are. I thought you'd stood me up." She stopped, her head pivoting side to side. "What happened to Dr. Murphy?"

"He's making his getaway."

Paula checked her phone. "We have seven minutes and thirty-three seconds before our chariot home arrives. Can I buy my award-winning nurse another vino?"

"No, thanks. Between the nomination, the champagne, and your awesome company, you've done enough. Tonight was such an honor."

Paula hugged her. "You should've received the Caring Kind Award a year ago. You are such an asset to our unit and my life."

"Thank you for your encouragement and for being my friend. I love you and my work."

"No tears." Paula tapped her phone screen. "This is our evening to celebrate you. Aw, man."

"Something wrong?"

"I'm just not ready for our night out to end."

Dana sank back against the sofa. "Trouble with the natives?"

"Jake has decided school is a waste of time. I'm tired of riding herd on him."

"Don't give me bad news. I always use your boys as standard measures for Sam."

Paula dipped her chin. "You better start a new search because Jake has dropped his standard in the mud."

"Motherhood is not for sissies. Sam is badgering me for a pet." Dana huffed out a breath. "It's all I can do to take care of one little girl. I don't know how you've raised two boys."

"A little bit of luck and a lot of love." She slanted a glance at Dana. "Of course, booze and friends help. Are you sure you don't want one for the road?"

"No, thanks. I need to be clearheaded in case there's an unwanted critter at home."

"It's too late anyway. Looks like our driver is Johnny-on-the-spot." Paula craned her neck. "Yep, a white Corolla just pulled up beneath the canopy."

Dana stood and lifted her elbow. "It was a lovely night. But I feel guilty accepting an award for a job I love. My patients give me ten times more than I can offer them."

Paula wove her arm through Dana's. "You're pretty special. You know that?"

"I know I have special friends."

"I saw you dancing with Dr. Murphy. You both looked kind of dreamy-eyed. What happened?"

The electronic doors opened, and the cool breeze fanned Dana's cheeks. "He's quite the charmer, even called this my Cinderella night."

She climbed into the back seat of their ride, and Paula slid in beside her. "Ooo, how romantic."

"I liked it," Dana said. "But just when I was starting to think he was a regular handsome guy, our star oncologist turned into a toad."

Paula's contagious laugh filled the car. Although Dana's underwear cut into her belly, she couldn't curb her laughter.

Man, she loved her girlfriend.

CHAPTER THREE

"What the heck!" Kyle blinked at the sunlight filtering through the faux wood blinds. He never overslept. And he *never* dreamed about women—until this morning.

"Great! Just freaking great!" The sheets entangled his legs as tight as the remnants of his dream trapped his thoughts. On the morning he really needed to come up with a treatment option for his patient, a woman occupied his mind. Why should he be surprised? Dana rarely followed the rules —at least when it came to dealing with him. Still, she didn't deserve his abrupt departure, especially on her Cinderella night.

Jeez, the stupid lyrics of that song had created an earworm to aggravate him. Despite the guilt weighting his shoulders, he stepped inside the shower and adjusted the temperature. The tepid water didn't do squat to cool his thoughts. Dana might be a hot nurse, but he wasn't going to start something with a vulnerable little kid in the mix. Been there, done that. Except his mother *had* found her Prince Charming.

"What is wrong with me?" he muttered. "Cinderella, and

now Prince Charming?" He only caught snippets of kid movies when he visited Pediatrics. Speaking of which, Joey had his first treatment today, and Kyle was late.

He jerked the towel from the rack, and the holder clattered to the floor, leaving a nice hole in the plasterboard. Super. Now, he'd have to call the manager to repair the wall. Like he was ever home to let someone inside the apartment.

Pushing the unsettling thoughts from his mind, he rushed through his morning routine and then navigated his bike's handlebars through the front door. At least the weather was nice. He swung onto the narrow seat. With a little luck his day would improve. Ten seconds after he parked his bike in the rack adjacent to the hospital, his phone rang.

He tapped the screen. "Dr. Murphy."

"It's Dana. Sorry to interrupt your morning, but were you notified Mr. Kramer died last night?"

"What?" He stumbled over the curb and recovered. "He was stable yesterday evening during my rounds."

Although in end-stage, Mr. Kramer had improved. Kyle planned to discharge him this morning so he and his wife could go home and discuss his next steps.

Kyle shoved his glasses against the bridge of his nose. What was he going to tell Kramer's wife? Not today. Jeez, not today.

"Paula's looking into it," Dana continued. "According to the night nurse, the resident said he was going to notify you. Paula has a call in for him."

"I'm on my way up." He cleared his throat of the odd raspy quality.

What a difference a day could make. Yesterday, he was closing in on the last month of his oncology fellowship, Triangle Oncology had reached out to set up a meeting, and one of the partners had stopped by his table last night. He snorted. It was merely to see if he planned to dance, but it was still contact. Today, he'd lost his favorite patient.

At the elevator bank, Kyle raked his hair from his face. He needed a haircut. Between his fellowship demands and extra shifts in the emergency department, his days were short of free time. When he slowed his breathing, the rapid thud in his chest slowed.

Stop reacting and think.

A good oncologist didn't address serious problems half-cocked. He knew firsthand about bad decisions. Although he was like a laser on cancer diagnoses and treatment options, he'd been a total bust in the family-relationship area. He was going to fix his problem—soon.

"Focus," Kyle murmured. "Did I miss something with Mr. Kramer?"

Slipping his fingers beneath his glasses, he massaged the bridge of his nose. He should've rounded again after the awards ceremony. *Should-haves.* Grandma Stella would be all over him if she heard the term. To her, thinking about what you *should have* done represented a colossal waste of time. Smart folks focused on *what is*. He needed to call her. Ryan said she loved his calls. The stainless doors glided open, and Kyle squeezed inside the crowded car.

His luck just kept getting better and better. Visitors and staff packed the elevator until he felt like cells on a slide. Worse, every light on the floor panel was illuminated. The stupid elevator would stop on every floor like the city bus halted at every street. Chill. Kyle thumbed through his messages. It never worked out to step onto the unit floor with a preconceived notion of what might have happened to his patient.

The Murphy Family Daily from his sister-in-law, Talley, blinked in his unread texts.

The elevator bounced to a stop on the second floor, and

he gripped his phone. Relax. Bad outcomes came from stressed-out decisions. Check out the home front. Though his finger trembled, he swiped his text screen.

TALLEY: Hope continues with teen attitude. A turnaround must be coming soon.

"WE WISH," he muttered. No surprise there. His little sister had pretty much run off the rails right before Whit's retirement.

The elevator dinged, and people shifted. Perfume strong enough to asphyxiate a horse stung his nose and made his eyes water. Without looking up, he stepped back until the handrail bit into his thigh.

TALLEY: You're going to be an uncle in the fall. Tried to call but went to voice mail. Try checking your voice mail once in a while.

CRAP ON A CRACKER! Talley was pregnant? Maybe she'd have a boy. His grin faded. A man couldn't go home after nine months of silence. He'd have to go sometime . . . but not yet. Once he nailed down an oncology practice and got his finances in order, he'd go home.

The elevator dinged for the next floor, and the sound seemed to stretch out like an ECG flat line.

The screen flashed with a text from the oncology resident.

"About time," he murmured.

. . .

DRAKE: Running late.

"YOU'VE GOT TO BE KIDDING!" Kyle's chin dropped to his chest, his hands tightening around his phone. Like he had time to help out the resident. Right. Did he carve time out of the extra emergency shifts, his patient caseload, or his sleep time? Kyle swiped the screen.

TALLEY: Nate's considering a career in the Navy.

HIS LITTLE BROTHER was another casualty after Whit's retirement. Kyle shifted again as workers exited and entered the elevator. He and his youngest brother had mooched from Whit's fame and fortune. Just thinking about it cramped his stomach. His little brother had to escape to the Navy just like he'd abandoned home for medicine. Nate had always followed him into trouble.

When the doors slid open on Six, he exited, thumbing his calendar. Rounds until eight. Tumor Board at nine.

"Oof!"

His shoulder crashed into a solid object, and he braced, dropping his phone. It clattered on the hard tile near a pair of white shoes. Dana bent, collected his phone, and handed it to him.

He might as well dig a hole because this day was on a downhill spiral.

"Thanks." He tapped the screen, and a photo of him with his three siblings flashed. "I don't think it's broken."

Silence.

He swallowed. Why was he surprised by her cold shoulder

after last night? Nothing should surprise him, considering his morning.

"Did the service call you about Mr. Kramer?"

"Your call was the first I'd heard about it." He'd like to think she cared enough to be aggravated about their evening's end. But that was just ego talking. One dance and a glass of wine hadn't caused her clipped speech and nervous glances.

"What happened?" And why was she gnawing her lip? He might be a jerk, but he didn't bite. "Kramer was stable. Although he refused the clinical trial I recommended, he had a good six months."

"It's *Mrs.* Kramer—" She huffed out a breath. "I'm worried about her."

Out of respect, he turned his head to give her time to regain control. But he didn't have all day. A text displayed on the screen. Joey's treatment had been postponed to later this morning, which gave him time to research what had happened to Mr. Kramer.

"I need to understand what happened with my patient." He softened his tone. "Drake hasn't updated me yet."

She seemed more at ease when he avoided constant eye contact, so he thumbed through his numbers for Drake's while Dana brought him up to speed. He paused on the Send key, unsure if he'd misheard her report. "Wait. Are you saying Kramer's body is still up here—in the room?"

He froze, and his heartbeat hammered in his ears. Could this get any worse? Without waiting for an answer, he turned toward room 610, avoiding a nurse wheeling a patient with wiry gray hair toward the elevator. That should've been Mr. Kramer heading for discharge.

Shoulds again. Shoulds and medicine were mutually exclusive. Stick to the case facts, the 'what is.' He'd lost a terminally ill patient six months early. His gut cramped again. Good thing he'd missed breakfast.

The paper taped to Kramer's door stopped his progression. Dana reached for the note, but he caught her hand and read: *Do Not Enter. Check at nurses' station.*

Last night, humor and interest shimmered in her wide-set eyes. Now, they were red-rimmed with spiky lashes. But no tears—for now.

"The note's a terrible way to handle the situation." She stepped back. "Mrs. Kramer hasn't answered her phone. I was horrified I'd miss her. What if she walks into the room without knowing her husband has died?"

The scent of cinnamon tickled his nose, and the refrain from Stealing Cinderella circled his thoughts. Life was precious. Kramer's life. His life. He liked kids. But casual relationships could go south in a heartbeat—at the child's expense. Actions always had consequences, and he had to think beyond *his* patient and *his* career. Mrs. Kramer came first.

"We'll work it out." He pushed the silver handle to enter Kramer's room.

When the door whispered closed behind them, the hairs along his forearms lifted. He shook off the strange sensation. It was a hospital room. He'd spent thousands of hours in them over the past six years. Why did it feel so...alien? Kyle jerked his hand through the hair that kept falling in his face.

Focus. Case facts: Lawrence Kramer, seventy-two years old, diagnosed with aggressive oat cell lung cancer with brain and bone metastases. Deceased.

Cold reality chilled him. Mr. Kramer no longer needed his medical skills. And Mrs. Kramer?

His gaze bounced from the curtained hospital bed to the striped sofa, the recliner, and the guest chair. "We can't tell her in here."

"The sitting area at the end of the hall gets the morning

sun." Dana's voice sounded small, like she was talking from a distance.

He lifted his hand toward her and then dropped it.

Get it together.

It was always tough losing a patient, especially the good-natured Mr. Kramer. The man was full of life despite his disease. And he and his wife? They were such a happy couple, like Mom and Ryan and Talley and Whit. Love like theirs was rare.

So why had Kramer stopped treatment? Had he screwed up? Missed a persuasive argument? The treatment he'd offered Kramer would've extended his life. But Kramer had kissed his wife's hand, smiled, and said no thanks. He was ready to go home.

But he hadn't gone home.

His widow would be here any moment. Kyle needed to review the case facts, so he could explain the unexpected death to her. On the tablet to the right of the door, he tapped the key to bring up Kramer's medical record.

Found unresponsive.

Heat singed his cheeks.

Do not resuscitate order. Time of death 02:42.

Kyle jabbed at the key to close the screen. "Great, just great."

Drake also needed a remedial documentation course. No, Drake needed more guidance, guidance that he hadn't provided to the resident. He adjusted his glasses on his face.

"The night nurse didn't have time to . . . tidy up." Dana's soft voice filtered through the privacy curtain. "I can't let Mrs. Kramer see him like this."

The sorrow in her tone tightened his chest. But with the thick fabric pulled around the bed, he could only make out her shadow. When Kyle moved around the curtain, air whooshed from his lungs like a popped balloon.

Dana was gently combing Mr. Kramer's hair across his brow.

"Kramer was a good man." Frustration laced his tone. At least it was better than despair. "He deserves dignity."

An unexpected flashback of his grandmother Rose's death thickened his throat. She'd also died from lung cancer. When he smoothed the pillowcase near Kramer's head, his hand shook. Had he talked too fast to the Kramer's? Maybe he should've called in social services, something. If he'd just understood the signs, maybe his patient would be dressed and ready for his wife to pick him up. Kramer had been excited about the impending discharge.

"Do we have to tell her the time of death?" Dana said.

He stared at the bed linen, feeling as useless as the discarded tubing.

"Will it matter? She's lost her life partner. He died alone." Because his doctor had been socializing.

When Dana bent to fold Mr. Kramer's hands over his chest, the moisture in her eyes sparkled from the light. She'd argued with him about hospice when he'd recommended cutting-edge therapies. Her passion for her patients equaled his. Dana Graham didn't just talk the talk. She'd seen something he'd missed. If he wanted to improve his skills, he needed to learn her technique.

At Kramer's bedside, she eased the tape from his lifeless hand and straightened the thin hospital gown. Her efficient movements equaled Kyle's, yet she handled each task as if she were swaddling a newborn.

He spent hours studying new drugs, new trials, and new treatment protocols. But what about the human aspect? The words from Dana's acceptance speech last night circled his mind: *Patients need more than treatments and diagnoses. They need kindness, a healing touch.*

He'd been so busy learning the science, he'd lost his

compassion. But he could still learn, change, and develop into the physician he imagined.

"Thank you for alerting me about Mrs. Kramer," he said. "You're right. The Kramers deserve a final act of kindness."

His words sounded as hollow as the lame excuse he'd used for last night's exit. He glanced her way. The gentle motion of her hand as she folded the sheet across Kramer's chest intensified his guilt.

"I'm sorry she has to learn about his death so late."

Not near as sorry as he was. Mrs. Kramer was too late—because of him.

When he twisted to move a chair near Kramer's bed, his arms felt stiff, unsteady. He glanced at Dana, hoping she hadn't noticed. She'd turned away to move tissues to the bedside table. Unbelievable. The woman thought of everything—anything to ease the situation for her patients and their families.

Nothing reduced the pain of losing a loved one. Some things you just didn't get over. Still, Dana's thoughtful acts might help Mrs. Kramer.

Pain throbbed behind his right eye.

"I failed them." Crap on a cracker, he'd spoken those words.

CHAPTER FOUR

Two hours later, Dana tucked Mrs. Kramer into her son's car and turned toward the hospital entrance. A gentle breeze lifted the loose strands escaping her ponytail and cleared her mind. Kyle hadn't failed, but she had. Although she'd supported the widow through her loss, she'd failed to support her colleague, failed to ask for an explanation for his practice philosophy. And last night?

Not everyone liked children. Her snap judgment stemmed from a bruised ego. She'd been attracted to Kyle, wanted to explore a relationship. He hadn't. She huffed out a breath. Time to right her wrong. Her mother's accident had taught her one very valuable lesson she hoped to never forget: tomorrow wasn't guaranteed.

When Dana exited the elevator on the sixth floor, Lynn, the unit secretary, looked up. "Have you seen Dr. Murphy? He forgot to sign a form for Mr. Kramer."

Paula stuck her head out of the medicine room. "He's on the pediatric unit."

"He's avoiding me." Lynn shuffled papers. "The docs hate the new form."

"Administration harped about the electronic records." Dana scrolled through her patient screens. "Then they added another document."

Lynn, a young woman who looked like she should still be in high school, raised her hands. "Don't shoot the messenger."

Dana checked the time. She could eat a little crow on her way down to lunch. "I'm on first lunch. I'll stop on Three and get his signature on my way down."

Within forty-five minutes, Dana had rounded on her patients, picked up her lunch, tucked the clipboard with the form under her arm, and marched to the elevator. She'd made inaccurate assumptions about Dr. Kyle Murphy in the past twenty-four hours. Maybe it was time to talk to the man. Not argue, have a conversation—after she apologized. They'd been locking horns since he'd started his fellowship at Wilcox Memorial. She shook her finger in the air, and the elevator rolled open.

"See there. More assumptions about what motivated him." It was time to ask him why he'd selected Wilcox. Ask why he threw treatments at his patients until something stopped cell growth. She understood the need for trials; she also thought they were too costly. Not just in monetary terms, but in mental and emotional deprivation. Science couldn't provide all answers, and every patient couldn't be saved—like Mom.

She bowed her neck and scrunched her face, trying to squeeze out the jagged edges of the memory. After two breaths, she opened her eyes to her scary reflection in the stainless door. Sam called it her crunchy face. Dana called it her coping mechanism.

"Gift check," she murmured.

She had the perfect job, a fabulous head nurse, and a

delightful five-year-old who made her heart sing. After today, only ten overtime shifts separated her from her financial goal to purchase a home. If she made a smart buy, she could take her little angel to Disney World. After four years of sacrificing mommy time for a nursing education, she couldn't wait for a vacation with her best girl.

The elevator bounced to a stop, and the doors glided open to cheerful giraffes, elephants, and monkeys dancing along the walls of the pediatric unit. Odd place for a man who wasn't a fan of kids.

"Where can I find Dr. Murphy?" Dana asked a nurse at the unit desk.

The young man pointed down the hall. "Playroom."

Dana snapped her mouth closed. Okay, she hadn't seen that coming. So did he have a friend or family member with a sick child? Or was he just taking a time-out in a happy area? She huffed out a breath. After their morning with the Kramers, a few stolen moments with a toy train might be just the ticket.

Whoa! A squeak leaked from her shoe at her sudden halt. To her right, a bank of windows separated the hall from a large, carpeted play area interspersed with beanbag chairs, books, games...and her oncology fellow.

Kyle knelt beside a wooden town, complete with curvy roads, and motored a toy car in front of a fire truck propelled by a five- or maybe six-year-old boy dressed in oversized hospital pajamas.

"Whoop, whoop, whoop! Move over, firetruck's coming," the boy said, his nest of messy blond curls shining beneath the fluorescent lighting.

When he leaned over to race his truck by Kyle, the gown slipped, revealing a port for intravenous medications.

"How can—" Dana bit off her favorite question. This situation required a kid tactic. "Volunteer Graham reporting on shift. Who's in charge?"

"Danny's the fire chief." Kyle moved to make room for her. "What do you say, Chief?"

"You can be a police officer like my mommy." The boy handed her a black-and-white car. "The fire's in the red house."

"Got it," Dana said.

"Were you looking for me?" Kyle asked in a low tone.

"I need your signature. Our admin was losing her mind because she's leaving early, and she hates getting dinged over missing documents."

"Varoom. Varoom!" Kyle moved his car through the inter-section. "Your volunteer fireman is reporting." He turned to Dana and whispered, "We have some great drugs for OCD. I could write a script for her."

"Errrrr. Errrrr," Dana mimicked a siren. "It's on the clip-board." She nodded toward the floor. "All you have to do is sign. I'll take it upstairs after my lunch break."

"Set up a roadblock," Danny ordered.

"Wow!" Dana parked her toy car behind the fire truck. "You're a great chief."

Danny shot her a heart-stopping smile, which added a flush of color to his pale cheeks. Dana nipped her bottom lip.

"Treatment time," a nurse in animal-character scrubs called from the door.

"Not yet." Danny's chin trembled, and a tear sparkled in the corner of his eye. "Mom's not here."

Kyle scooped up the boy and gently positioned him on his shoulders. "Watch your head, Chief. I'll keep you company until Mom arrives."

Dana's heart stuttered. With the boy perched on his shoulders, their differences in medical ethics seemed unim-portant.

In the infusion room, Kyle eased Danny into a child-size lounge chair in front of a game console. "What's it going to be, buddy, TV or game?"

"You should wear a little boy more often," she said.

Kyle winked. "Danny's the man!"

Actually, Kyle was the man. She'd just been too busy bumping heads with him to notice. She was noticing now. Noticed how his smile comforted the boy. Noticed his long gentle fingers when he exposed the port. Noticed his easy banter directing Danny's attention to the console and away from the treatment.

"And look who's here just like she promised!" Kyle waved his arm to the side like a circus ringmaster.

"Mom!" Danny brightened.

Kyle fist-bumped Danny's knuckles. "I'll check on you tonight, okay?"

Outside the room, Kyle scribbled his signature on the form. "I thought this was a paperless hospital."

"Almost." Dana returned the pen to her pocket. "That's probably why you missed it."

But she'd been the one missing the dinosaur in the living room—mainly Dr. Kyle Murphy. At least she'd missed this side of him. For months, she'd focused on his up-front, in-your-face race for every treatment known to man. Dr. Murphy never gave up. Even when it was time to let go.

"Mind if I join you for lunch?" The low timbre of his voice blanketed the ding of the elevator.

I mind—a lot. Especially with the way her alien body was reacting to him. However, she still owed him an apology and a conversation.

"Sure." She checked the time. "But my lunch break is over in twenty minutes."

They squeezed onto the elevator stuffed with Wilcox Memorial staffers breaking for the cafeteria. Since he'd turned to wedge into the small parting of bodies, they were face to face. She stared at the lapel of his lab coat, intrigued by the faint hint of sandalwood and starch. Kyle spared time to drop off his lab coat to the cleaners. Impressive.

Since she brought her lunch, they separated at the cafeteria. Dana hurried to the patio, eager for fresh air and blue skies despite the chilly April weather. Once outside, she didn't bother to crank open the red umbrella or unpack her peanut butter sandwich. Cheerful daffodils bowed in the North Carolina sunshine, and the earthy scent of spring replaced the caustic odors of disinfectant. Dana inhaled and lifted her face to the sunlight, trying to forget about the soothing scent of sandalwood and the rarity of starch.

"Perfect." Kyle slid his food tray across the table's metal surface. "Outside, not my lunch selection."

"Grilled cheese and fries?" Dana unpacked her sandwich. "Should be pretty safe. What's Danny's prognosis?"

"Good. His dad is a bone-marrow match."

"Thank goodness."

"Yeah, good news. But the family is strapped financially. That's why I went down. Mom's working two jobs and runs late on Sundays."

"I'm sure Danny and his mother appreciate your thoughtfulness. How'd you know about him?"

"Danny's mom came in after an auto accident to talk to a suspected drunk driver." Kyle opened a ketchup packet. "While her suspect was in X-ray, we started talking. She told me about Danny, and I offered to help out."

"Funny how life works." Dana tore her sandwich into two pieces. "You offered to help Danny, and I offered to help out Lynn, which led to a few minutes with Danny."

"Kids are great mood elevators. They also keep life in perspective."

"You were great with Danny and Mrs. Kramer."

"Thanks. I always feel better after a visit with Danny." He shook his head. "But Mrs. Kramer? I didn't feel great after talking to her."

"You were there for her," Dana said.

"But his life didn't have to end this way. Kramer was a perfect match for a trial I found." He broke eye contact and fisted his hand. "I promised I'd always offer hope, but I couldn't convince him to enroll in the trial. He wouldn't even give himself a chance."

"He made the best decision for him and his family." Like she'd made the best decision for Mom.

He was already shaking his head. "Cancer is not synonymous with death. Medicine has made huge strides in the past decade. Look at Danny. We used to lose every boy like him. Now, some types of leukemia have almost an eighty percent remission rate."

"But we don't have all the answers." Medicine couldn't save her mother's brain injury. "Especially for second-round treatment. It's okay to stop treatment to spend the final days surrounded by family at home."

"But Kramer didn't get home." His voice echoed in the silence.

"What makes you think a trial would've changed his outcome?"

She'd seen patients suffering through trials only to die in a hospital bed instead of home with loved ones. She'd also cared for Mom.

"At least he would've had a chance." After a pause, he raked a hand through his hair. "I've been rethinking my presentation. I had the best options, but I didn't present those options to the Kramers in a way they could understand."

He wadded his napkin and tossed it on his plate. "Have you heard about using artificial intelligence in medicine?"

Dana shook her head.

"It's pretty cool. The trials are fed into the computer. The machine reads and sorts the information and then lists potential treatments for the patient."

He leaned toward her, his elbows resting on the mesh wire of their table. "Physicians still review the data and determine treatment. But there are hundreds of ongoing trials. With AI, I get a targeted list for my patients."

She must have frowned because he started talking faster and with more intensity. There was nothing wrong with his passion in determining the best treatment. She sat back against her seat.

He stiffened. "What?"

This was the in-your-face Dr. Murphy she knew, the superficial view he showed to the world. But she'd joined him to apologize, not critique his presentation skills. Too bad more people didn't know the man she'd seen in action today. Arrogance didn't motivate his behavior. She'd known physicians who considered death as a personal defeat. But an egotistical doctor wouldn't help prepare a body for family viewing, hold a recent widow against his chest, or distract a child awaiting treatment. Dr. Murphy cared about his patients—deeply.

He was staring at her, his dark brows merged above the top of his glasses. "Feedback would be appreciated."

Well, feedback was difficult sometimes. "Have you heard of the sandwich-critique method?"

He pushed his uneaten meal toward her. "Were you interested in my grilled cheese?"

"I agreed to meet to apologize."

"For ...?" He winked. "Not wanting my leftovers?"

OMG, she'd never known the similarities between a

grown man and a five-year-old. But she would not be diverted. "For the Dr. Frankenstein label and for thinking you made decisions based on ego."

He blinked. "Dr. Frankenstein is nothing, a joke for Nurse Ratchet. The ego thing is harsh."

So much for sandwiching the good comments over the not-so-good ones. "Sorry." She raised her hands. "That was my original impression and the reason for the apology. I unfairly judged you. After talking to you, watching you with Mrs. Kramer, I was wrong. With Mrs. Kramer, you were amazing, compassionate, and patient. The same with Danny. You didn't push. But when you were talking about AI..."

His squint buried his dark eyes in his paintbrush lashes. "Too strong?"

"Almost scary. I'm a professional, and I haven't been recently diagnosed with a grim disease."

He shoved his glasses up his nose. "That's why I wanted to talk to you. I knew you had something I needed to learn."

"You've already got the technique. Tap into the Dr. Murphy who talked a scared little boy into his treatment and consoled a grieving widow."

His mouth scrunched from side to side. "That bad, huh?"

"I wouldn't consider your AI delivery a friendly persuasion."

It was like flipping on a light switch. He straightened, and his eyes gleamed.

"But don't you see? AI changes everything. I study the science and know the data. Patients select me for my skills. But AI? It's the extra hours I need to sleep at night. The machine can process hundreds of documents. I'm good, but not that good."

She crossed her arms over her chest. "I take back the part about your ego."

He smiled, sending his eyes dancing. "A man's got to know his strengths."

"And his weaknesses."

"That's why I need someone like you."

When he clasped his hands on the table, she guessed it was his way of toning down his boundless energy. The man could keep pace with Sam, and her five-year-old spun on an endless energy source.

She tapped the screen on her phone. "I'm flattered, but—"

"I don't want to be an average oncologist. I want to be the best I can be."

"Why?"

He sat back. "I'd think that would be obvious."

"Not to me. What made little kid Kyle decide to be an oncologist?"

"Little kid Kyle couldn't find his bottom with both hands."

"Moms are experts at detecting a diversion."

He shrugged, which was a delaying tactic.

She tapped her phone. "We have eight minutes and twenty seconds."

"Is this a test?"

"My time is limited." She raised her index finger to cut off his response. "Right now, I'm working at least one extra shift a week. Today was number ten. When I finish, I'll have a nest egg for a down payment on my own place and a Disney vacation."

"I'm down to twelve." He nodded. "I work extra in the ED to pay off my student loans."

"Great. We understand our priorities."

"So you'll help me?" He scrolled through his calendar. "We could meet for lunch and dinner if we're pulling doubles on the same day."

She tapped her phone. "Five minutes."

"Thirty-minute breaks might not be enough. What about after work?"

"Sam does not meet male friends."

He stopped scrolling and pinned her with his gaze. "Ever?"

"So far."

"And her father?"

"Is not in the picture and won't be—ever."

Something about Kyle changed. She couldn't identify it, but she'd learned to trust her instincts, especially when it concerned Sam.

"I know why you protect your daughter. My mom remarried after Dad was killed in Afghanistan." He held her gaze. "That's why I cut out last night. You're a package deal. I'm not in a position to handle with care."

She hadn't seen that one coming. So was she angry or disappointed? At least he was honest.

"Last night..." He picked at the mesh table. "Adults understand about breakups. Kids don't."

"Very astute." But she couldn't focus on her feelings, not with him staring at her. "Now, why oncology?"

He shoved his plate to the side. "A patient once told me he thought his life was over after diagnosis, so every day after was a bonus. Every day counted, meant something, despite his diagnosis. He said a part of him died that day. But something else lifted him up, made him appreciate every morning. I wanted to model his life. Be around people with a similar outlook. Learn from them. Help them."

Dana curled her fingers around her lunch box to keep from touching him. "That's what keeps you going, fills your well during emotional droughts like today. It's not the reason for your initial decision."

The man had a fierce frown, but she'd already uncovered

his soft underbelly. She narrowed her gaze to win his stare-down.

He huffed out a breath, and she nearly shook her fist at the sky.

"Do you ever give up?"

She smiled. "Do you?"

Although the right side of his lip twitched, he didn't smile. Too bad. He had a nice smile. The expression eased his intensity.

"My dad was a hero." He held her gaze without blinking. "He gave his life for his country. I'm the oldest of four. Each time he deployed, he took me aside. I was the man of the family. To honor him, I needed to do something important. My younger brother has amazing physical abilities. I'm smart. I preferred pediatrics, but the reimbursement is dismal. I loved genetics, cytology. Oncology was a good fit for me."

"But not the only fit. Why oncology?" She tapped her phone. "In three minutes or less."

"What about thirty minutes at the coffeehouse down the block." He raised his hand. "Just thirty minutes."

If she limited it to thirty minutes, she'd still have time for Sam's bike ride. Since it was T-ball season, her daughter would be practicing before dinner with Dad.

"Thirty minutes. But only if you answer my question."

His expression was so filled with exasperation, she almost laughed. But, hey, Sam had made her an expert in patience.

"Do you know what it's like to lose all hope?" he said, his voice low.

Her breath rushed from her lungs. "Yes." But her voice sounded far away. Too bad the hurt wasn't.

His features had softened. He understood. But she hadn't. Hadn't really understood her need to know what drove this complex man. Shared pain. Deep inside, she'd identified a kindred spirit.

She cleared her throat. "My mother and sister were killed in an auto accident a year ago. Robin was killed instantly. Mom was in a vegetative state for almost a year." A year of getting up and moving through life when a huge part of her was missing. "There was no hope for her recovery. Dad... couldn't let her go."

CHAPTER FIVE

K yle entered the clinic through the side door. Unlike the hurried atmosphere on 6-West, the staff greeted appointments, took vital signs, started infusions, and drew specimens at a slower pace.

His heart rate slowed within moments. He loved oncology, loved the science, loved finding the resolution to a problem, finding the right treatment for the right condition.

"Afternoon, Dr. Murphy." An elderly gentleman with wispy white hair stepped on the scale.

Kyle nodded, silencing the patient's treatment scrolling in his head. Did he scare his patients? A cancer diagnosis was scary. Facing the unknown was scary. But, according to Dana, people interpreted his enthusiasm as scary. If Triangle got the same impression, they'd never offer him a partnership. How did a guy fix that?

He jerked the chart from the back of the exam room door. His patients entrusted him with their lives during a very vulnerable time. He had to know more, do more. But changing his professional personality in thirty-minute segments with Dana? Women were tricky. Science was black-

and-white. Wild cards could always pop up, and science could evolve. But one could count on it.

People always seemed to blindside him. Just when he thought things were cool, bam. He'd screwed up, and everybody was ticked off. Like with his brother Whit. He figured Whit liked the fame and fortune. He never considered Whit only played professional football to subsidize his medical education. Crap on a cracker, he better not have to change more than just his professional perspective.

By the time Kyle arrived at the coffeehouse, Dana was already sitting at a small wire table for two beneath the green awning outside.

She lifted her drink. "Chop-chop, doc. Clock's starting."

Of course it was. "I'm starving after my dismal lunch. Want anything?"

She tapped at her phone. Yeah, yeah, he'd hurry.

At the counter, he paid for his order, picked up utensils, and joined Dana. She sat with her head against the back of her chair, her face tilted toward the sun. A weird sensation settled in his gut. Must be hunger pains. Good thing, he'd purchased the croissant and a carton of milk.

When his chair scraped the pavement, she straightened and tapped her phone again. "Twenty-four minutes and counting."

"Pretend I'm a new patient." He handed her a fork. "You're Dr. Graham. Explain an AI treatment."

When she looked up at him, with the sun highlighting the fiery tint to her hair, the urge to kiss her washed through him. He forked a bite of the pastry. The flaky layers drizzled with chocolate and sliced almonds filled his senses, but he'd bet she was sweeter. Her smile faded, and he gripped the fork to keep from feeding her. Anything to return the sparkle to her eyes. She had amazing blue eyes.

Off task, Murphy.

Distractions caused mistakes. And Nurse Dana created a monumental distraction.

She rolled her eyes upward and rocked her head side to side the same way his little brother used to do. "I didn't realize I signed up for a test."

"I need an example."

"Mr. Murphy."

"Kyle."

"Don't talk down to patients." She cut a small piece of his croissant with her fork. "If you're Dr. Murphy, they need a 'sir' title. In the hospital, we take away a patient's clothes and their routine. The least we can do is balance the power scale every time we have a chance."

"I just spent the past twelve years in school to earn my medical degree."

Her brows had arced and not in a good, sexy way.

"Yeah, yeah, yeah," he said. "Point made. I guess I don't have to go by *Dr*. Murphy."

"Mr. Murphy," she started again.

Her soft but precise voice swept through his head as easily as the pastry slid down his throat. Both caused his lips to bow upward. If his patients had the same impression, they wouldn't learn a thing about AI.

"So, Mr. Murphy, why don't you and your wife talk over your options? This treatment has a good chance of giving you more time. I can't predict how long, but your body responded well with the first round of treatment. However, only you can make the final decision. Take your time. If you or your family members have questions, write them down, and we'll talk tomorrow."

She smiled.

"Well, heck." He sipped his milk. "Where do I sign?"

Her laughter floated on the breeze and made him smile like a fool. He couldn't help it. With the vivid blue sky above, her smile, and a belly full of croissant, he felt better than he had in months.

Still, an oncologist had more to consider than a brief education. "I like the idea about writing down questions, but I'm not always available to talk the next day. Plus, the faster we initiate treatment, the better our chances in obtaining remission."

"A few days isn't going to change an outcome, and it can mean minimizing patient stress. Doesn't stress exacerbate disease?"

So did excessive weight, genetic and environmental factors, but—

She was squinting through a microscope, and he was the specimen on her slide. "Okay, point taken, teacher."

She removed a Spring Fling flyer from her purse. "Are you coming?"

"I'm trying to impress Triangle Oncology. All partners participate in hospital and community events. I'll be there."

"Paula's on the committee." Dana dazzled him with her smile. Her parents must have spent a fortune in orthodontics —unless she was genetically lucky. "Kyle?"

He chugged his milk and closed the carton. "If she oper- ates the Spring Fling like she does 6-West, Wilcox will generate enough money to fund a new wing."

Okay, what was wrong with his response? It wasn't like the Wilcox fundraiser was going to get his patients into remission.

"She wants two more docs for the dunking pool."

"No way." He shook his head. "I volunteered for a dunking pool during my undergrad days. I'm not the Speedo type. Plus, they fill those tanks with a water hose, so it's freezing."

"How about a kissing booth?" The corner of her lip twitched. She was messing with him.

"I'll volunteer for something, but not the dunking pool."

She tapped her phone. "Oops. Got to go. I've got a girl waiting for a bike ride."

"Thanks. This was just what I needed." He'd always learned faster by doing, and Dana was the perfect teacher. And she wasn't hard on the eyes. He collected the trash. "Are you working a double tomorrow?"

"Just days." She stuffed a napkin into her empty cup. "Sam has a T-ball game."

"Fun. She must be under seven. The age group cracks me up."

Her narrowed gaze snapped his jaw closed. What? Did he have food on his teeth or something?

"Sam is five," she said like he hadn't just talked about the age group.

It wasn't like he invited himself to her game. "When I was in undergrad, I umped for the county. It didn't pay a lot, but the kids were great. I can't say the same for the parents. Man, some of the dads lost their minds if their kid didn't hit the ball. In T-ball, no less."

She was staring at him. He swallowed. Why was he running his mouth? She didn't care if he'd been a T-ball umpire.

"I rechecked my financial goal." *Close your mouth, Murphy.* "I should hit it in about twelve more ED shifts."

Jeez, where was his head? He dumped the trash into the waste can near the entrance. It had to be her eyes. Every time she looked at him that way, his brain shut down, which was insane. She was a woman. He'd dated quite a few in his thirty years. "A friendly competition might make the overtime more palatable."

Did she have any idea how cute she was? Dana wasn't some fake beauty model. She was more the girl next door, the girl who made a guy laugh, feel good. Except when she stared at him like he was one crayon short of a full box.

He shrugged. "No wager involved. I can't wait to have free time again." Come on. She had to miss free time too. He'd been working extra shifts for over three years.

"We'll see."

"What does that mean?" But she'd already turned toward the Wilcox garage.

She wasn't the only single woman in the hospital. That nurse in the ED had come on to him last week—if he needed a date. He didn't.

The Wilcox elevator opened on Six. She'd been clear that she didn't introduce her daughter to a man. It was a good practice. Except when he was the man. In the meantime, he had patients to see.

As he scrolled through his patient list, a memory surfaced of a little boy with missing front teeth. He'd whacked the ball all the way past second base. Umps weren't supposed to cheer, but he steered that little guy toward first base and had to stop himself from following him around the bases. He'd bet his next paycheck Dana never had a problem running the bases. She was having no problem running from him.

Although he wanted to quiz her some more, figure out why she was hot and cold when it came to him, he had patients. Mr. Harris and his son were waiting for him. One look at the pair told him the impending conversation wasn't going to be easy. He glanced down the hall. Too bad Dana wasn't working. This would be the perfect time to practice her latest lesson. Not that he doubted he could pull it off. He'd like to show her he'd paid attention. Although he wasn't making headway with her, he was a good physician. And he'd master his touchy-feely side.

He forced a smile, which was a little harder than he antic-ipated. He'd never been a smiley kind of guy. Although happy enough, his education required time and intensity. If he'd gone into communications, maybe he'd smile more.

"Hey, Doc." Mr. Harris raised his hand. "This is my son Mark. I've already made up my mind about the trial we talked about, but Mark wanted to talk to you."

"What can I answer for you?" Where was Dana when he needed her? She'd be impressed by his use of a question. Plus, he was smiling. Of course, he couldn't do her soft, lilting tone, but he couldn't help his larynx was bigger and produced a louder, deeper sound.

Mark shook his hand. "Dad says he's going home soon."

"If his counts continue to improve, I can discharge him the day after tomorrow." Kyle scrolled through the electronic chart. "He'll need to return next Tuesday for his first outpatient treatment."

"He says he's not entering the trial."

Kyle stiffened. Yesterday, his patient had agreed to the treatment. "The trial is a perfect match for your cancer. With treatment, you could stay in remission for six months or longer."

Harris slowly shook his head. "I've had enough treatment. I want to go home and spend time with my granddaughter."

"Didn't you hear him?" Mark said, his face red. "With treatment, you'll have six months, maybe longer."

"And what's that going to get me?" Harris jiggled the tube running oxygen to the nasal cannula. "Carly's playing ball tomorrow, and I can't watch her. I can't take her fishing, can't work in my garden. Why do I want six more months of sitting in my rocker and coming in for treatments?"

"Six months, Dad! That's more time. Listen to me. Listen to your doctor. This is crazy!"

While Mark argued with his dad, Kyle checked the bedside table for the statistics he'd recorded for Harris. The science was solid, the genetic testing matched— *Listen*. That's what Dana did. Listening was one of the differences between his approach and hers.

Kyle scooted a side chair near Harris with a scraping noise that set his teeth on edge. Although Kyle wasn't as tall as his famous brother, he was pushing six feet. Regardless, he didn't want to hover above Harris. Dana said he needed to get on his patients' level.

"Gentleman?" He raised his hand.

Mark raked his hand through his hair. Harris crossed his arms over his chest. How did he get through to this guy? "What can I do right now to make this better?"

Harris narrowed his eyes. Great, his patient didn't trust him. Jeez, he really did need Dana's help. If not her, maybe he could enroll in one of those touchy-feely courses.

"Your granddaughter is playing tomorrow," Kyle said. "Outside or inside?"

"It's one game," Mark insisted. "She's six. It's not like it's the Olympics. I'll bring Carly by the hospital as soon as the game's over. She can tell you all about it."

"I don't want five minutes *after* her game," Harris said. "I want to see her play. Cheer for her."

"First," Mark said through gritted teeth. "you're still in the hospital. Even if Dr. Murphy discharges you, it hasn't rained in weeks. Remember the last time I took you to a game? The dust was so bad, you couldn't breathe. I thought we'd have to bring you to the emergency room. And you weren't as sick as you are now. How do you think Carly would feel if she thought her game made you sick?"

Tomorrow, Kyle had planned to pick up another shift. "I'll take you to the game." Crap on a cracker, he'd lost his mind. But it could work. If he were dying, he'd want to see his granddaughter play. Like he was ever going to have a grand-daughter.

He stood, which was against Dana's recommendations.

But if he didn't move, he might detonate. "It's perfect. I love watching kid games. If you have problems, I'll be there to help."

"You'd come with me to the game?" Harris said.

"Only if you buy dinner." Kyle smiled, and this time it wasn't forced.

"I'm still not going to agree to the trial."

Kyle lifted his palms. "No strings. But I would like you to reconsider." If he showed Harris he could still enjoy a quality life, maybe he'd change his mind.

His son was shaking his head. After the game, maybe both would reconsider. As for Kyle, he'd get to watch a game—outside. How long had it been since he'd had a few moments of fun outdoors? Jeez, he wasn't any better off than Harris. They'd both been stuck in the hospital too long.

Harris crossed his arms, again. "I guess I could think about it."

At least he hadn't said, *we'll see*. Kyle held up his thumb. "Give me the time and place. Tomorrow, I'll write your discharge orders and pick you up thirty minutes before the game. After the game, I'll drive you home."

"We can drive him home," Mark said. "As long as you're with him during the game, you know, if he has a medical problem."

"The game starts at seven." Harris's lip twitched.

The sly old fox was enjoying this, which was okay. Nothing wrong with a little fun.

"I'll be here at six forty-five to give you time to load up your belongings."

Harris tapped the open suitcase on the bed. "Just don't be late."

Kyle resisted the urge to salute. "No, sir. We'll be there for … What does your granddaughter play?"

"T-ball. Last year, she hit the ball into the outfield."

"And ran to third base instead of first," Mark muttered.

Harris smiled. "That's why we have coaches at every base."

It was good to see Harris's smile. His patients with positive attitudes always responded better to treatment. Plus, he got it. He imagined a little girl racing down the baseline. Did Dana's daughter have her smile? He blinked. What were the chances Dana's kid played ball at the same park?

"Dr. Murphy?"

"Call me Kyle. We're baseball pals now."

Harris frowned and shook his head. "I'm old school. I'll call you Doc for now. If Carly gets a hit past the bases, I'm treating you to a hot dog and beer."

Kyle bumped his patient's frail fist. "Deal."

CHAPTER SIX

A t the stop sign near her home, Dana closed her eyes and inhaled. What a day at the hospital! She hadn't stopped all day. Which hadn't pleased her new student, especially since she also couldn't meet him after work. A neighbor pushing a small dog in a carriage waved and stepped onto the curb. Dana lifted her palm and accelerated through the crosswalk.

No more work thoughts. She'd done her best to help her patients today. But work was over, and family time was beginning. Gratitude check. She had a wonderful, healthy little girl, a loving, supportive father, and a comfortable place to live. Her Corolla bumped over the entrance to Dad's driveway. Soon, she'd purchase her own place.

The car's tires crunched on the gravel drive leading to the backyard. Tucked in the corner, beneath a giant oak, sat the small green cottage she and Sam called home. Although Dad loved having her literally in his backyard, she yearned for her own place. Dana wanted to claim the same milestones her sister had. With the purchase of a home, the struggling little sister image would be gone. In ten more shifts, she'd have enough for a down payment—if she could find something affordable in a good school district.

The screen door slammed the minute she parked beside the cottage. "Mommy!"

Dressed in her red *Tigers* game T-shirt and navy shorts, Sam plowed into her.

"Hey, sprout. Did you have a good day at school?"

"Yes, ma'am. And me and Grandpa practiced. I'm going to be a star today."

Sam followed Dana into their cottage, chatting nonstop about preschool. "Tomorrow is pet day, except I don't have one."

Dana removed her uniform and pulled on a pair of cutoffs. "Pets are a big responsibility. Mommy is gone at work during the day, and you are in school."

"Grandpa's here."

The soft fabric of her *Tigers Mom* T-shirt settled across her shoulders. "Grandpa isn't asking for a pet. When you turn six years old and show me you can take care of a pet, we'll start looking for one."

Sam's bottom lip protruded. "That's a long time."

Not near long enough. With her schedule, time progressed at warp speed. Soon, her little princess would ask for a car. Unlike a pet, a car didn't snare heartstrings.

"Grandpa's fixing pancakes." Sam propped her chin on her fists. "He says we have to eat early for my game."

Thankful she'd dodged the pet bullet, Dana poured a glass of iced tea. "Did you do something kind today?"

"Not yet."

"Why don't you think of something nice to do for someone else while I take my fifteen-minute rest time."

Sam scrunched her features as though she were considering the plight of the Western world. "What about our bike ride?"

Dana tapped her phone screen. "Since we have a game—"

"Nooo. You promised. Grandpa pumped our tires."

Dana raised her palm. "Back up there, sprout. It's rude to interrupt."

"But you were going to say no." Tears filled her daughter's eyes. "You promised."

"Wrong answer." Do not look at her crocodile tears. Good moms remained calm and determined. Sam was such a special girl, one Dana wanted to grow into a caring adult, not spoiled and demanding.

Sam side-eyed her.

"I bet Grandpa could use a big hug." Dana settled into the ancient recliner. "Hugs make him happy."

While silently counting, Dana scrolled through her texts. Twenty seconds passed. Sam gave a dramatic sigh and shuffled toward the kitchen. No doubt, her daughter was checking the digital clock on the microwave. Moments later, the cottage door closed. Dana hid a smile. Her girl was whip-smart.

Dana snorted at an incoming text. Three miles away, Paula was bumping heads with her youngest son.

DANA: The trials and tribulations of single moms.

Paula: We must unite. Sending a virtual glass of red.

THE COTTAGE DOOR opened and closed, and Sam returned to the kitchen.

DANA: I'll spike my tea.

Paula: Gotta go. Referee required!

. . .

THROUGH HER PERIPHERAL VISION, Dana tracked her daughter's progress. Sam parked at the counter, propped her hands beneath her chin, and stared down the clock. She knew the rules. If she broke the fifteen minutes of silence, she'd lose her bedtime story.

Another text signaled. Dana tapped the screen. Holy crap!

KYLE: Wanted to tell you at lunch. ☹ Successfully used your technique with Harris. Thanks, teach. ☺

SHE THUMPED HER CHEST. OMG, she was not getting full of herself over one compliment. Her lip bowed. It was kind of sweet. She should've known Dr. Murphy was serious about learning new communication techniques. The man didn't do anything halfway. Although he'd probably be better off with a professional communications coach, a gal could always use some praise.

Of course, if he'd witnessed her five-year-old's behavior, he might reconsider her communication skills. Speaking of ... Dana tapped the timer on her phone. Five minutes down, ten to go. What seemed like forever to Sam was rapid to a working mom. Leaning back in the chair, she let her eyes drift closed.

"Time's up!"

Dana blinked.

Sam's nose touched hers. "Time's up."

She'd actually slept ten minutes. Dana grabbed her phone and sent Paula a text.

DANA: Power nap!

. . .

DAD PUSHED OPEN the screen door when Dana and Sam returned from their bike ride forty-five minutes later. "There's my baseball star and super nurse. How was the ride?"

"We saw baby ducks!"

"Okay, chatterbox." Dana toed the kickstand. "Wash up. You can tell Grandpa about our ride during dinner."

Sam raced down the hall, still talking.

"Scrambled-eggs-and-pancake night." Dad removed the pitcher of pancake batter from the refrigerator. "I'm trying to avoid a stomach upset."

Settling into the comfortable partnership of cooking with her dad, Dana removed the griddle from beneath the counter. Although GI issues had never been a problem for Sam, her mother had been adamant about light meals prior to games. Old patterns were hard to break.

"Did everything at work go okay today?" He glanced down the hall. "Better tell me quickly before Sam monopolizes the conversation."

"Isn't that the truth?" Dana retrieved a spatula. "I was once concerned about her delayed speech."

Dad cracked eggs into a bowl. "I believe she's well past that milestone. And your day?"

"Nothing earth-shattering. We were up to our knees in alligators. I didn't even get a lunch break. Did I tell you I learned something new about Dr. Murphy?"

"Is this the man with the Dr. Frankenstein title?"

Dana cringed. How could she be so mean? "I should practice what I preach to Sam. The label was unkind and untrue."

Dad poured syrup into a pitcher and placed it in the microwave. "So, how did he redeem himself?"

With the intoxicating aroma of maple syrup and browning cakes filling the kitchen, Dana shared the events in less than two minutes, ending with the thank-you text from Kyle.

"They're clean!" Sam raced into the kitchen, her dripping hands thrust in the air.

"Towel, Sam."

"You said wash up."

"Washing up includes drying. Now, hurry up. Pancakes are almost ready."

The recent events continued to circle Dana's thoughts through the rapid dining on pancakes and packing the car. With Sam spinning another preschool episode, Dana buckled her seat belt.

"Would I like him?" Dad settled into the passenger seat.

Dana couldn't blame her brain freeze on the bump from Sam kicking the back of her seat. But she wouldn't insult Dad by pretending ignorance.

"How'd you know I was interested in him?"

"I met your mom in college. All she talked about was basketball. Annoyed the dickens out of me. Sometimes annoyance covers the first seeds of attraction. Besides, she had freckles across her nose and a gaze that pierced through me. We were totally unsuited for one another. But those are the relationships you have to watch."

She was watching Kyle Murphy, all right. But she was more concerned about the way the man dominated her thoughts. Of course, his latest texts had facilitated that occupation.

"He texted me a thank-you for helping him talk to a patient."

"His mother obviously taught him manners." Dad glanced at her. "That's a good thing."

Kyle wasn't the only one who had learned manners. "Thanks for all you do. Managing Sam, work, and school would be impossible without your help."

She held up her hand. Instead of slapping it for a high

five, Dad wrapped his calloused fingers around hers and gave her a little squeeze.

"You and Sam are my life."

"And you're ours." Thank you, thank you for this day filled with the people she loved.

She kept her eyes on the road, afraid she'd tear up if she met Dad's gaze. At dinner, Dad had been a little sad. She'd lost a mother and sister; Dad lost his life partner and a child. A child! Her grip tightened around the steering wheel. She couldn't think about ever losing Sam.

"I'm going to whack the ball." Sam kicked the back of Dana's seat so hard, the seat belt cut into her belly.

The sun had lowered along with the temperature by the time Dana turned into the entrance to the county park. Newly leafed pin oaks lined the asphalt and testified to Raleigh's nickname of the City of Oaks. Since cars filled the designated parking area, vehicles lined the grass adjacent to the baseball fields. Dana found a vacant spot and parked.

The minute the car halted, the click and snap of Sam's seat belt filled the silence. "I see coach and Teddy."

"Don't forget your glove...and your hat," Dana said.

Sam raced across the grass while Dad removed the cooler filled with juice boxes and orange halves from the trunk. Together, they lifted the cooler for the walk to their assigned baseball diamond.

"I know you've almost saved your down payment," Dad said.

"I'm getting close."

"We haven't talked about it ..., anyway I wanted to tell you not to worry about me."

She glanced his way, but his gaze had settled ahead in the distance.

"I'll be okay," he continued. "I love having you close, but a parent's greatest accomplishment is to launch a child into the world. I'm proud of you and what you've achieved. Don't hold back on my account."

Dana's grip on the handle slipped. "I wasn't, I mean—"

"I love you, and I love helping every way I can. But I don't want to smother you." He stopped beneath an oak adjacent to their assigned field.

The ice sloshed inside the cooler along with her thoughts. Had she sounded ungrateful? She loved him. She wanted him near, wanted his support. It's just she needed ... what? To stand on her own.

"It's a perfect evening for a ballgame." He pushed the cooler close to the trunk and turned toward the car.

"Dad?"

When he turned to her, the tenderness in his smile brought tears to her eyes. He lifted his arms and she stepped into his embrace.

"No need for tears." He motioned toward the car. "I'm proud you have the will and the opportunity to spread your wings."

Maybe that was it. She wasn't a child. "You aren't smothering me."

They walked arm-in-arm to the car, and she noted the slight variance between the height of her shoulders and his. He stopped at the open trunk, handed her the two folding chairs, and removed the portable table that would hold the team snacks. "Poor word choice. I just don't want you to alter your dreams because you're worried about leaving me alone." He slammed the trunk closed. "I miss them every day. But we're moving forward, one day at a time."

She adjusted the chairs and hurried to catch up with him. "I keep thinking I'm going to wake up, and the terrible ache will be gone."

"Sometimes I talk to her like she's still here, or the phone will ring, and I think it's Robin, calling about her latest game."

"Mom and Robin would've loved watching Sam play."

"That's what makes life worthwhile."

On the other side of the field, Sam chased a ball. She bobbled it, scooped it up, ran halfway back to her coach, and then stopped to throw it.

"We're working on the basics," Dad said. "I thought she understood, but it looks like she's still determined to run the ball to the infield."

Dana blinked back the remnants of her tears; laughter always eased her heartache. Her daughter was amazing. Watching her grow was a gift—that would go too fast if she didn't force herself to slow down, savor.

She found Dad's large hand and squeezed. "We're doing a great job with her. I'll always need your help. Sam needs a grandpa." Especially since her daughter would never have a dad. That one was on her. But better no dad than a bad dad.

"That's the thing about family." His tone had lost its earlier sadness. "We may cry and moan on the silly day-to-day differences, but we always stand together. If you won't let me help with the Disney vacation, consider letting me help with the down payment."

"I always considered buying my house as a rite of passage. To me, it says I've accomplished something big. Something for me and Sam. I'd like to purchase our first home on my salary. But I appreciate the offer." She hugged him. "I also reserve the right to change my mind, especially with the increase in housing costs—and you know it has to be nearby." Unless— "Wait a minute. I didn't even consider you might need the cottage for something else."

Dad's lined features crumpled in confusion.

Maybe not. Dana shrugged. "You never know when you might need the cottage for a sexy widow."

Dad hooted, and a parent toting a portable love seat stopped and stared.

"I married the woman of my dreams and raised two wonderful daughters and one amazing granddaughter." He shook his head, but a fleeting shadow crossed his gaze. "I'm not in the market for lightning to strike twice."

"If someone special comes along and you need the cottage to entice her, let me know."

He wrapped his arm around her shoulders, and for a moment, she was a little girl again, and he was her protector and provider. He was always bigger than life. But Mom's accident had taken a toll on him. His shoulders, once broad and solid, stooped. The months spent knowing there was no hope for recovery and waiting for Mom to die had broken his heart both literally and physically.

She shaded the setting sun with her hand. "Looks like there is room on the bleachers to sit if you don't mind the sun."

On the diamond, the opposing teams started warm-ups, and the three rows of bleachers slowly filled with parents. Although bystanders and coaches occasionally occluded their view, Dana preferred the first row so she could encourage Sam. What mom could resist her sweet daughter in her baseball uniform, even when it consisted of an oversized T-shirt and shorts? With her cap cocked to the side and pigtails hanging down her back, her little girl was cuteness overload. Dana would develop bilateral cheek cramps if she continued to smile like a fool the entire game.

Sam was on deck when the only other girl on the team raced from the bench to the coach. Her small chubby hands jerked a helmet over her low-banded ponytail.

"Whack it, sweetheart!" a raspy male voice called from her right.

She hadn't met Carly's parents yet, so—

Dana blinked. Guiding her patient from Room 625 to the bleachers, Kyle held Mr. Harris's elbow as he eased onto the metal bleacher.

"Comfortable?" Kyle parked the miniature oxygen tank at Harris's feet.

Dana blinked again. They were right there. She could literally reach out and touch Kyle or Mr. Harris. It didn't make sense. When Kyle looked up, his smile outshone the sun, which was crazy. How could he plop down beside her and smile like it was just another day at the game? To her knowledge, Kyle—no, Dr. Kyle Murphy—had never attended one of her daughter's games. And he couldn't just look like another dad. A dad? Dana waved her hand near her face. She should've snatched one of the extra juice boxes. The night was heating up instead of cooling down.

"What are the chances?" Kyle thrust his hand toward her dad. "You must be Mr. Graham. Kyle Murphy. I work at Wilcox Memorial with your daughter."

"Shhh." Harris waved a hand at them. "Carly's teed up again."

Dad shook Kyle's hand and then turned toward the game. Dana forced her frozen neck muscles to operate.

At the plate, Carly wiggled her bottom and rotated her feet, sending up a small cloud of dust.

"Just like you practiced," Harris murmured. "You can do this."

Carly wound up and *whack!* The ball sailed toward first base. Like the crowd, Carly straightened and watched the ball. Then, instead of running, she jumped up and down.

"Run, Carly!"

Harris's words must have stimulated the father/coach at the plate. He leaned down and pointed toward the base. Carly sprinted toward first, the bat still gripped in her hands.

Her teammates on the bench shouted, "Run! Run!"

Carly dropped the bat halfway. When the ball landed behind first base and rolled toward second, the first-base coach motioned Carly to run to second base. A little boy in a yellow Mustang T-shirt watched the ball rolling to the outfield. A defensive outfield coach directed the fielder to get the ball. In the meantime, Carly hustled to second base. The Tigers on the bench jumped up and down, shouting for Carly to run. Harris was on his feet, cheering along with Kyle.

When the second-base coach held up his hands, Carly stopped. The outfielder threw the ball toward home. At least that was the intent. The ball went straight up and landed a few feet in front of the boy.

"I love watching these games," Kyle said.

His laughter, rich and deep, muffled Dana's hearing. She shook her head. Maybe she should cut back on extra shifts for a while.

"Did you see that?" Harris shouted. "That's my grand-daughter. She's a spitfire."

"Dad!" The coach at home plate clasped the wire fencing installed to protect fans from the ball. "Take it easy. You just got out of the hospital."

"She's awesome," Harris said.

"I agree, but—"

"I've got my own personal doctor right here. You need to turn around and coach the team." Harris motioned for the coach, who was apparently his son, to return to the game.

Dana needed to stop thinking about Kyle's transformation. It was darned hard. The intense physician she worked with had morphed into a regular guy. With his sunglasses, his laser-eyed focus didn't cut into her. Dressed in faded jeans and an open-collared blue shirt, he could be any dad.

"Batter up!" Harris clapped his hands. "Bring her home, batter!"

Sam approached the plate, the batting helmet lopsided on her head.

Dana straightened. "Whack it, Sam!"

"She must be yours." Kyle leaned closer.

She had to quit reacting to him. He was a physician on her team, not a date. Her shoulders drooped. What was wrong with her?

"Bring her home, Sam!" Dad cheered.

Dana clenched her fists. Her daughter was up at bat. How could her beautiful little girl grow so fast? At the plate, Sam whirled in a circle and nearly tripped over her feet. Yep, definitely her girl. Dana had hoped Sam would get her mother's sports gene and miss her klutzy one.

"Take it easy." Dad gentled his voice. "Look at the ball, just like we practiced. Perfect. You don't have to pound it. Just meet the ball with the bat."

Crack! The ball sailed over Carly and the second baseman's heads.

"Woo-hoo!" Dana leaped to her feet. "Yay, Sam! Run!"

Sam dropped the bat and bounded for first base. Carly was already churning toward third, and Harris's son rotated his arm like a sideways copter, signaling Carly to run home.

"Go, Sam!" Dad cheered.

Dana caught herself before she leaned toward Kyle. Thank goodness he was watching the field. She turned to Dad. "She hit it."

"Of course she did."

"This is her second hit of the year." It was bragging, but a mother had to support her daughter. "Go, Carly. Go, Sam."

With her ponytail swinging side to side against her narrow back, Carly zeroed in on home plate. Dana snorted. The little girl was almost as focused as Kyle on the floor. The home-plate coach picked up Sam's bat to clear the baseline and stumbled. Carly, intent on running home, plowed into her dad. Out of the jumble of arms and legs, Carly scrambled to the plate on hands and knees and slapped the pentagon with her hand.

"Safe!" she hollered.

The crowd laughed until the coach stood, holding up his right foot.

"Are you all right?" Harris called.

"Just sprained—wow!"

Kyle hurried around the barrier and steadied Mark. "Since you can't bear weight, you should probably get it checked out."

"What about the game?" Carly said.

The parents assisting at the bases converged around Mark and Kyle. Sam sat on third base and drew in the loose soil. The high-pitched voices of the kids in the dugout settled over the field. While two men helped Mark off the field, Kyle stood behind the plate.

"Play ball!" Kyle turned to Harris. "I'll drive you and Carly home after the game if Mark doesn't make it back. I texted the ED. They're backed up this evening, but my colleague said he'd watch out for Mark."

In the meantime, Dana would watch out for Kyle. The take-charge trait she'd witnessed on the oncology floor transitioned into a competent coach on the field—except it was different. Instead of steely-eyed progress at any cost, Kyle leaned down to talk to each batter. He lined up the younger team members with the ball and showed them how to adjust their hands. He praised, he encouraged, and he facilitated the smooth operation of the game with the rambunctious kids.

"I like this man," Dad said near her ear.

Dana straightened. Had her study of Kyle been obvious? She touched her lips. At least she'd kept her mouth closed. Just the thought of gaping at him in front of the parents and kids heated her cheeks. The overhead lights blinked on. Now, even the field mocked her.

She liked Kyle too, but she couldn't say that to Dad. "I haven't seen this side of him."

"He's good with the kids."

He'd been good with Danny. Would he be good with Sam? Dana swallowed—hard. Foolish woman. There would be no big Disney vacation or home of her own if she sacrificed her extra shifts for personal time. And an activity with Kyle Murphy would definitely fall into the *personal* category.

CHAPTER SEVEN

U nder the glow of the overhead lights, the Tigers shuffled through the red dirt to high-five the opposing team. Kyle rubbed at the ache in his cheek. How long had he been smiling? Not that he could prevent it. For him, kid vitality always infected him like a rampant virus. A virus he'd been missing in his life. In the last few years, time constraints had forced him to stop coaching. Maybe next year. Next year?

On the bleachers, Harris smiled despite the disease eating him from the inside out. Next year wasn't guaranteed. Harris had fought for one more game. Kyle had avoided his family for too long.

"Don't squish it!" Carly's high-pitched voice pierced the low chatter of the kids huddled around a caterpillar.

Kyle straightened. He was supposed to improve his patient communication skills, not lose his perspective on personal goals. He was not going home until he could pay his brother Whit in full. End of story. Sure, life didn't give guarantees, but he only needed six months to accumulate the money and get his life in order. Whit should live another fifty years. His family didn't understand his absence, but they'd get over it when he returned. On that day, he was heading back to Sunberry with a check. His tail might be between his legs, but he'd hold his head up.

In the meantime, these little kids were having a good time and he wasn't going to spoil it. He'd always loved picnics and family baseball games. As a teen, he'd craved peace, quiet time without the constant noise rumbling through the Murphy home. Right now, it sounded . . . fun.

Just get over yourself!

He joined the parents and kids forming a line in front of a portable table. Dana wrapped orange halves in napkin for each child. In a lawn chair beside her, Harris handed out juice boxes and high fives to the team. Color had replaced his patient's earlier pallor. His gaze sparkled with interest, and a broad smile hid his gaunt cheeks. Harris looked better tonight than he had in weeks. Fresh air and kids could do that to a man. It had worked for Kyle.

It also worked for Dana. With her rosy cheeks and smile, she made the perfect team mom. Of course, the ball cap helped. Although she'd been stunning dressed to the nines at the gala, game-mom Dana radiated energy, a trait he couldn't ignore.

Jeez, what was the matter with him? He'd taken an evening off in hopes Harris might reconsider the trial. His schedule didn't allow for a social life. Still, he'd made a heck of a trade for Harris and himself.

Kyle hung back to let the team collect their snacks.

"Did you see Jimmy smash the caterpillar?" a little boy with spiked hair said. "I told him to catch it for my hedgehog. He loves to eat them."

Carly made a face. "Jimmy wanted to see if the guts were the same color as the outside."

Kyle snorted. He could listen to their high-pitched antics all day long. Although Carly made a spectacular hit, the glory of the moment was long gone. Now, caterpillar guts occupied her and the boy's attention.

Harris held out a juice box. "Good game, good game." He hugged a giggling Carly. "You made the bat crack so loud it hurt my ears."

"Nah, Grandpa!"

Harris gave Caterpillar Boy a box and lifted another toward Kyle. "Juice?"

He waved his hand. "Anything stronger in the cooler?"

"Sorry." Dana's ponytail, pulled through the hole in the back of her cap, swished across her back.

"I think I owe you a hot dog and beer," Harris said.

"Sounds good. I'm also giving you and Carly a ride home." Kyle checked his screen. "Mark's in X-ray. They don't think his leg is broken, but the ED is busy, and he's not sure how much longer it will take."

"No problem," Harris said. "I'm free for the rest of my life. Besides, this is a perfect night for our favorite postgame place."

Carly stopped, orange juice dripping from her chin. "Jimmy's Night?"

"After that great game?" Harris stopped the juice trail with his thumb. "Absolutely. I'm treating the team to ice cream."

"We're getting ice cream!" Carly shouted.

Leave it to a kid to possess the treat radar. The caterpillar guts were surpassed by the shout, ringing like a dinner bell through the small band of kids.

"Jimmy's Night!" Mr. Graham announced to the line of parents waiting for players.

Fifteen minutes later, Kyle followed the caravan of parents to a redbrick strip mall. Two miles from the park, the famous Jimmy's, a locally owned restaurant, featured a game room, miniature golf course, and go-cart track. Kid haven.

Inside, Harris approached the counter and purchased ice

cream and game tokens for the players. Although Kyle and three other parents offered to share the bill, Harris declined.

"He needed this." Dana spoke from his right.

"Nights like this are why we live." Kyle lowered his voice. "This outing came from an awesome nurse who has special powers."

"Really?" Her gaze sparkled from humor and the overhead lighting.

"I know. It's the weirdest thing. I spent years learning the science, and she just waves her wand."

Her brows raised. "There's a wand involved?"

Man, she was cute. "Insane, right? Who would've thought, right here in Raleigh?"

"Are you angling for another pearl of wisdom?"

He picked up his order. "Nah, her idea worked so well for my patient I figured it might work for me too. I took tonight off."

Curious thing about putting the science brain to rest, it allowed other parts of his anatomy to surge to the surface. Parts that could threaten his objectives. He ignored the threat. Tonight was for fun.

He snaked through the parents and kids to the end of a long wooden plank table. He stepped over the bench seat across from Dana and her family. George Graham was involved in a long-winded story with Harris about the need for more youth teams. Carly and Sam debated if gummy worms or multicolored sprinkles created the best ice cream topping.

"Mind if I join you?" he said.

"Sure, but it's going to cost you." Dana angled her head toward his tray.

"French fry?"

"Thought you'd never offer."

He pushed to stand. "Do you want some?"

She plucked a golden-brown fry from his basket. "No. I'll share. I'm not greedy, just collecting on a small debt."

Kyle settled back on the bench and reached for the ketchup. He squeezed hard, and the rude sound cut through the chatter. The kids erupted into giggles and reproductions of the noise.

"Way to go." Dana plucked another fry from the red plastic basket.

"That's the beauty of kids," he said. "Life is unfiltered, and they laugh at things adults consider embarrassing."

She bit into the fry, drawing attention to her plump upper lip. The surrounding chatter diminished as Kyle's geek mind launched. The orbicularis oris encircled the mouth. But it wasn't an ordinary muscle, just as Dana wasn't an ordinary woman. Four complex quadrants interlaced to give her mouth an appearance of circularity. What were Dana's other layers?

"I don't have cooties."

Kyle blinked. In front of him, Dana twirled a fry. The mouth that had sucked him down an anatomy-lesson rabbit hole had lifted into a wry smile. He straightened.

"Work?" she said.

Truth or lie? "Um, kind of." That wasn't exactly a lie, but it was also a long way from the truth. He wasn't going to confess where his mind had really gone.

"'Kind of'? In our profession, 'kind of' isn't really an answer."

"Busted. I zoned out."

Her expressive brows lifted and then pulled together over the top of her pert nose. She had a cute little nose. It was straight and a bit thin but tipped up at the end in a sort of so-what attitude. It fit her personality, at least what he knew of it.

Her tongue moved beneath the very lip that had mesmerized him.

"Do I have food on my teeth?"

"Smile." He swallowed his groan. "You have a great smile." And his stupid comment erased it from her face.

"You are a tricky man to read."

"Mom!"

Dana lifted her index finger and gave her daughter the mom-look. "Excuse me."

"Excuse me, Mom?" Sam tried again.

"Mr. Harris bought us tokens. Can I play the bowling game?"

Mr. Graham stood. "I got this. Nice meeting you, Kyle."

"It was good to get away from the hospital," Kyle said. "Sam, that was some hit you made tonight, and your throw to second saved a run. Thanks for letting me coach your team."

"You can come to my games—" The pint-sized Dana scrunched up her face, emphasizing a pert nose matching her mother's. "When do we play again, Mom?"

"Thursday evening."

"Thursday," Sam said. "I'll be even better because my grandpa coaches me after school."

"The more you practice, the better you play," Kyle said. "I have to work Thursday, but maybe I can come another time."

"Yeah, Mom works a lot too." Sam brightened. "But we're going to Disney World, just me and Mom. But we still ride bikes."

"Sam!" Spiked Hair hollered from the entrance to the game room. "Carly just scored a triple!"

"Gotta go."

"Every time she talks about me working, this huge guilt complex develops right here." Dana thumbed her chest.

"When we were kids, Mom renovated office space so she could take us to work with her. Can you imagine four kids dragging her down? I'd get so mad at my brothers. Mom did everything for us, and they still wouldn't listen. Of course, I was no saint. At the time, I thought I was this big helper, Mom's protector."

"Were you the oldest?"

"Yes, and a big know-it-all. The world according to Kyle Murphy. I don't know how Mom put up with me."

"Four kids. Wow, she was a miracle worker. It's all I can do to get Sam to make her bed and clean her room. And then I have to bribe her."

"Oh, there was bribery involved." Kyle sipped his drink. "But she did it. We were loud and a huge pain in the—" He lifted his brows. "Mom rarely raised her voice. Matter of a fact, sometimes she'd almost whisper."

"I'll have to try that one." Dana snatched another fry, her gaze distant. "I envy your big family. Paula talks about picnics and holiday dinners with her aunts and uncles. Sam will miss out on family gatherings."

Big families were fun, but he already had the sad trip down memory lane. From the little vee between her eyes, she didn't need another dose of sadness.

"Sam's got a great grandfather. I would've loved to have a grandfather play ball with me. Plus, you've got backup. After my grandmother died, my mom was on her own."

"I have many gifts."

"I was just wondering." *Keep it to yourself, Murphy.* He ignored the silent caution. "You seem to have a good relationship with your dad, and I'm sure Sam likes him nearby. Why the push for your own place?"

"For me." She rested her chin on her fists. "It's like a rite of passage. Every time someone asks where I live ..." She shrugged.

"God bless the child who has his own?"

"Exactly."

"I want to be debt free when I land a partnership."

"So you work the ED to pay off your student loans?"

Kyle sipped his beer. He usually liked a cold brew after a hot day. His lip curled from the taste as bitter as the idea of confessing his little brother had ponied up for most of his education, but loans were loans. In his case, he just wanted to hand Whit a check and be guilt free. Same concept as Dana's goal, with a twist. Everything in his life seemed twisted.

"Yep." It wasn't a *total* lie. He'd paid for the last semester of medical school—after Talley's enlightenment. He was so close to banking the funds to pay off his little brother, he could feel the relief. On the day he finally went home, he planned to hand Whit the keys to his car and a check for his education. His hand tightened around his glass.

Dana lifted her lemonade. "So here's to our freedom."

When she studied him like that, he struggled to maintain her gaze. Mom and Talley had the same effect on him. It was like they were staring into his soul, checking out his inadequacies. Which was insane.

"Are you interested in a race to the finish line?" He shrugged. "Kind of like a team effort. It makes it a little less tedious if you have a teammate to cheer you on."

Based on the slow lift of her lips, she was warming to the idea.

"No specifics required." The last thing he wanted to do was admit his debt. "We could check in by shifts. In a dozen shifts, I'll attain my benchmark."

She straightened, a sly smile curving her pretty mouth. "I'm two ahead of you."

This was going to be fun. "Exactly my point."

Her eyes narrowed as though she were adding numbers in her head. "It wouldn't hurt to add a shift to pad my account. I love my little car, but it's over the 100,000-mile mark. Two months ago, I had to buy a new radiator." She made the cutest face. "Did you know the bugs you hit at night break down and create holes in your radiator?"

"Ah, no. I can't say I've run across that tidbit in med school."

"Life lesson." She winked.

Kiss her. Kyle straightened. Good thing he only had a dozen extra shifts left. He was starting to suffer sleep deprivation. He swallowed. Maybe it was sex deprivation. Well, that wasn't going to happen with Dana. Five-year-old alert! He lifted his empty glass.

"Back to continued efforts." Stop swimming around in her gaze. "Are you working tomorrow?"

"Same time, same station."

"The test results should be back for a new patient. I want to get this right."

"You're serious about wanting my..." She circled her finger in the air. "Advice? This is different than the competition you suggested," she added, her playful tone gone.

"I spent my life learning science. I couldn't get enough of it. One topic always led to another. In the process..." What? "I don't know. You made me realize I'm missing a piece. Harris validated that tonight. Anyway, I need to sharpen those skills to be the best I can be."

"Being the best is important to you."

"If I can give Harris one more day with Carly, I've done my job."

"Who do you want one more day with?"

Since he'd drained his beer, he sat back. "My dad. I quit playing ball after he was killed. At first, I just helped Mom. I had two brothers and a sister. Hope was a toddler and a mess. My brothers...I guess they were shell-shocked."

"Mom!"

The child's cry cut through the din of voices. It was probably nothing, except Dana was moving, her features ghostlike. Sam? The sobbing girl plowed into Dana's middle.

"She fell near the bowling machine," Carly explained. "She's all bloody."

Kyle peeled Dana's arms away from Sam. "Let me have a look. Hey, Sam. It's going to be okay. I promise."

The wailing stopped, and Sam sniffed.

"Show me where you're hurt. Is your head okay? I don't see anything."

Although there was a lot of blood, most wounds were superficial. Kids could bleed like stuck pigs. And, often, moms lost it. He'd seen his share of hysterical moms in the ED.

Tight against her bloody T-shirt, Sam cradled her right arm. Kyle reached for it, and the girl backed against Dana.

"I'll be careful," he promised. "I just need to look. I don't think blood is scary."

"You don't?" Sam sniffed.

"Nope. For me, it's kind of like caterpillar guts."

Sam's lip twitched, and she let Kyle turn her forearm.

Somewhere above him, a gasp split the silence. "Is she okay? I'm the manager."

"He's a doctor," Mr. Graham said.

"Wow!" Kyle turned Sam's arm, revealing the three-centimeter gash along her forearm. "You're going to have a great story to tell your school friends tomorrow. They'll think you're the coolest kid in the class."

"I need to take her to the emergency room," Dana said, her voice shaky.

Tears welled up in Sam's big eyes, matching her mother's.

"Nah. Not necessary. Sam's a big baseball player, but that place is scary." Kyle lowered his voice. "I've got a bag of good stuff in my car. I keep it just in case ballplayers get in a wreck. I guess this is more of a bowling wreck, but I can fix you up. Will you let me help?"

Sam nodded.

Kyle squeezed Dana's trembling fingers. This was not the cool, calm nurse he worked with. But it was her daughter. "You can trust me, Dana. I'm good at this."

She moistened her lips and nodded.

"Okay, team. Finish your game, and Sam will be right back. And be careful around the bowling machine." He turned to the manager. "Check it for sharp edges. If you've got some duct tape, that should help until the owner can get it fixed."

Outside, he popped open the hatchback on his Subaru and sat Sam on the floorboard. "Mom, why don't you sit beside her?"

He'd never talked to Dana on a mom level, but something about her fear made him go with his gut. The last thing Sam needed was for her mother to lose her mind. Best to treat Dana like she was any terrified mother.

In the back, he reached for his medical kit. "I stopped for a bad wreck in my third year of med school. Since that day, I've kept a kit in my car. It's no traveling ED pack, but it works for minor injuries."

Silence. He pushed a bottle of normal saline into Dana's hands. "Make yourself useful, Mom. Open this."

Her silence was starting to worry him. Surely she wouldn't pass out and smack her head on the parking lot. Then he'd have two patients.

"Okay, Sam. I'm going to clean off the blood. After that, I'll dry off your skin. I won't touch your boo-boo." He held up a package of Steri-Strips. Sometimes the glue burned. "These are like Band-Aids, except they don't have cool characters on them. What's your favorite action hero?"

"Spiderman." Sam's voice was soft and shaky.

"Really? He's my favorite too. Okay, this may be a little cold." Kyle poured a capful of saline over the wound.

Sam's little arm shook, but she didn't move away.

"Good job. Be sure to tell your friends how brave you were, okay?"

Sam nodded.

"Now, this is very soft, and it won't stick to your ouchie. I'm just going to dry the skin so the strips will stick, okay?"

"Okay."

"Good job. Gosh, I wish all the girls who came into Emergency were as brave as you. I'd probably win an award or something."

"My mom won an award."

Kyle applied an adhesive to the wound margins. "She did. I bet you were proud."

"I stood up in front of the class and told everybody about it." Sam's voice was steadier.

A small noise sounded above him. He glanced at Dana. She'd lost the glassy-eyed look.

"Wow! I don't think I could stand up in front of the whole class. You are really brave."

"Yep."

"Are you ready for some magic?"

Sam nodded.

"I'm going to touch this strip to the edge of your boo-boo —like that—and close it up. One, two, three, done."

Since Sam had encountered a sharp edge, the wound margins were clean and approximated without a problem.

A tight smile creased Dana's feature, easing the pinch in his neck. Working with kids came easy, but the parents? They could be tough, especially when a child has a serious injury.

Sam lifted her arm closer to inspect it. "What about that place?"

Kyle squinted at the proximal end beneath Sam's finger. "There?"

"I can see blood," Sam said.

Kyle bit the inside of his cheek to maintain a straight face at the minute red. "Good eye. Lucky for me, I had you to point that out. I would've missed it."

"I don't want anything to fall out," Sam said.

"I see what you mean." Kyle opened another package and applied a strip to the edge. "Okay, sport. Why don't you and Grandpa go inside to tell your friends you're A-OK? Me and Mom will clean up the mess." Kyle caught George Graham's gaze and tipped his chin. The older gentleman nodded.

Sam's chatter faded, emphasizing the silence of the well-lit lot. The aroma of tomato sauce and sausage peppered the air. Now what? Did he talk to her, hug her? Sure, Murphy, that would work. Until the past week, she'd barely spoken to him, other than to disagree. He collected the packaging and huffed out a breath. Best to treat her like any other mom.

"Are you okay?"

"I'm embarrassed. I've never panicked before."

"Great kids like Sam don't grow on trees. Of course, you were worried."

He stuffed the trash into the side of his bag and froze. The real worry was how much he wanted to take her in his arms and redirect her worry.

CHAPTER EIGHT

4:59 A.M.

Dana blinked at the blue numbers on her bedside clock. Gratitude check. One: a very long night of fighting the futon's lumpy mattress had ended. Two: the minor wound from last night's tumble with the bowling game had not interfered with her daughter's sleep. Three: a new day was dawning to give her twenty-four hours to make amends for yesterday's backslide.

So what happened last night? Trained professionals didn't usually fall apart—especially in front of Kyle.

She switched on the overhead light in the bathroom and avoided the mirror. The woman occupying her body couldn't be Dana Graham. The Dana she knew had moved beyond fear. Experienced Dana had survived countless episodes of life with an active daughter: Sam falling from her bike. Sam "flying" from the porch railing. Each time, Rational Dana had dried Sam's tears, patched her up, and carried on like normal —until last night. Last night was a repeat of the months after the accident. Why had she regressed?

By 11:45 A.M., work on 6-West had forced the troublesome thoughts aside. Three discharges and two admissions in a two-hour period could do that to a nurse.

Dana pushed a wheelchair into Room 622. "Ms. Bowman, your chariot awaits."

Dressed in a flowered blouse with a matching scarf tied over her balding head, her patient beamed. Life was good.

Although her smile stayed in place, Mrs. Bowman parked frail hands on her hips. "I'm perfectly capable of walking to the hospital exit. Matter of a fact, it would feel amazing to walk out of this place. No insult intended."

Dana locked the brake. "None taken. But the Wilcox administration kind of loses their minds when patients don't follow the rules."

"I'm only complying so my favorite nurse doesn't get in trouble."

Ms. Bowman settled into the chair, and Dana handed her a small white bag. "I give one of these to every patient I wheel to the exit."

"What's this?"

"A little something for your send-off." Dana released the brake. "Have you got everything?"

"My husband has already loaded my things in the car. He even beat Dr. Murphy here this morning."

Dana pushed the chair into the hall. "Sounds like a celebration is in order. But first, discharge instructions."

After the quick review, Dana turned the chair toward the elevators. Good thing Ms. Bowman had her back to her because Dana couldn't suppress the huge grin splitting her face. With every rustle from the bag, her heart rate increased. Wait for it . . .

The hum of the kazoo echoed in the hallway, answered by a rhythmic clap. The administrative assistant stood at the counter. The bag rustled again, and Mrs. Bowman shook the miniature tambourine. Paula stepped from her office, clapping. With every step closer to the elevator, a patient or staff member lined the hall.

"I'm going home!" Ms. Bowman shook her tambourine and blew the kazoo again.

The elevator door slid open, and Kyle stepped to the side. "I didn't want to miss your send-off."

When Dana wheeled Mrs. Bowman inside, he discreetly tapped his wrist. Dana swallowed and nodded.

Fifteen minutes later, Dana parked the empty wheelchair and walked to the cafeteria. Standing near the entrance, reading his phone, Kyle was hard to miss. Since a hank of hair covered the top of his glasses, she guessed he was reviewing patient records. Her spirits tanked. She hoped there was no bad news in store for her patients today.

"Test results?"

He looked up. Why did guys always get the epic lashes? The answer clicked in her brain. Testosterone. For the conversation she had planned, she could use a dose, thank you very much.

Kyle stuffed the phone into his pocket, the semblance of a smile bowing his lips. "The Talley Murphy Daily News."

"Your sister?"

"Talley is my sister-in-law."

"What a great way to stay in touch. So, she lets you know how everyone is?"

"Pretty much."

Based on his scowl, he must not think it was nice. That was just wrong. He had a family, brothers and sisters, people who cared.

And she was not going to judge. Dana forced a smile. Supposedly, a smile changed your perspective. "I love that she takes the time to stay in touch." *Fake it till you make it.* "Your family must be close."

Silence. She glanced to her right and a lab technician

moved past her. She turned. Two steps behind her, Kyle stood in the dining room entrance. Staff veered around him, but he remained immobile. Had he forgotten something? Other than gratitude for his family.

She waved her hand six inches in front of his nose. "I thought you were hungry."

He blinked and nodded like Sam did every morning when she had to awaken early.

"Starving," he said.

Good for him. He could have her sandwich because it wasn't going to help unknot her insides. She had to get through this, or she would be irritable all day. Besides, a judgmental attitude did not feel or look good on her.

At the food line they separated. While Kyle scrounged for lunch, she secured their usual table. Routine soothed her—most of the time. She had to do this. It was the only way to progress. She'd had enough time to work through her issues. Like there was a timeline to slog through grief. Perched on the table, her unopened lunch bag mocked her. So, was she going to sit and let the iron-mesh chair dig through her bottom, or was she going to be the mother and person she'd promised to be?

Kyle walked toward her with two sugar cookies and a sad cup of chocolate pudding.

"Nice lunch." She dug through her bag. "Do you want half of my sandwich?"

"Nah, but thanks. I'm going for a sugar high today."

She bit into her sandwich, which wasn't too bad. She'd forgotten about the sliced strawberries she'd added to the peanut butter. "Let me know how that works out for you."

"How was Sam this morning?"

"Perfect. Mom always swore kids bounce." But she hadn't.

"Everything okay?"

The low timbre of his question eased the whirling

thoughts in her head. She swallowed some water from her bottle. "I need to apologize."

Whoa, she'd said it. That wasn't hard.

"For?"

She pointed both index fingers at him. "Hold that thought. This may sound convoluted." No, she was convoluted. But she was moving. "After Robin and Mom died, I was a mess. Two healthy people had been taken from me. That was bad enough, but I got this compulsion to protect Sam."

Kyle had stopped eating, his laser focus on her. Sometimes his intensity overwhelmed her. Today, it...comforted her. It was like she was the most important person in the room.

"You're a mother," he said. "Mothers protect children. Totally understandable."

"Yes, but I was a mama bear on steroids. I gave new meaning to helicopter mom. I was Momzilla."

His smile gently eased the tension in her shoulders. "I didn't see a Momzilla last night. Just a concerned parent who loves a special little girl. Sam's a cute kid."

"You were great with her." It was her performance that had gone awry. "I'm apologizing and telling you this as much for me as you. I didn't like last night's mom, but I need to forgive myself for the backslide so I can move forward."

Were his eyes glazed over? She leaned closer to him. He blinked, and his lip twitched. He was probably wondering if she were dangerous.

"I warned you my logic was shaky. But I can't be a loving mother, daughter, and—" She snapped her jaw closed. OMG, she'd almost said lover. She cleared her throat. "I'm working on forgiving myself. No judgment. No criticism. I just own the mistake or misstep, forgive myself, and strive to improve."

"How's that working for you?"

There was no humor or judgment in his tone or his intense dark eyes. Man, he really had great eyes. It wasn't just passion burning there, but compassion. This man cared and felt deeply.

"Actually, very well—most times. Last night caught me off guard. But I'm a work in progress."

"From this side of the table..." He spooned the last of the pudding into his mouth and swallowed. "I think you have an amazing perspective, and your patients benefit from it. Despite your loss, you always look for the ray of sunshine."

And he'd just showered her in it. But he was talking about Exterior Dana. "Sometimes I have to close my eyes and pray. My patients teach me to live in gratitude, not in fear. I try to focus on the little things to make me feel happy and alive. Things like the smell of Sam's hair after a bath. The warmth of her arms around my neck. A family dinner with Dad and Sam chatting us up until we want to tear out our hair." She forced a smile. "Sam's smile when she hits the ball, even if she doesn't always run to first base."

Kyle's laugh mingled with the birdsong.

Her face relaxed and joy lifted the dark cloud shadowing her thoughts. *Like talking about her fears and her blessings with him. Or the way his laugh growled from his belly.*

"Anyway, I have to work at being the person you described. It doesn't come naturally. Trust me, I was such a nut job even Sam and Dad couldn't enjoy life."

"Everyone has moments they aren't proud of."

The fine hairs at the base of her neck lifted. Based on the distant quality of his voice, Kyle might need a lesson in self-forgiveness too.

His phone alerted with an incoming text.

"6-West?" she guessed.

He tapped the screen. "Talley forgot something."

She shook her hands at the sky. "I love it! Please, answer her."

"Nuh-uh. I don't start conversations with Talley."

Really? That made no kind of sense. But he looked like his favorite puppy had run off.

"That's terrible." Dana added a bright smile to soften her criticism. "Send her an emoji just to let her know you got it."

"She knows." He returned his phone to his pocket. "Besides, if I respond, she'll start nagging me."

Dana leaned in. "So, what's your deep, dark regret?" *OMG! She did not just say that.*

His sister-in-law sounded like a great person. There had to be more going on here—if he would share. Considering the man was stiff as a board, it didn't look likely. It was sad to have a big loving family and not enjoy them. She could write a dissertation on regrets, regrets she could do nothing about. But he could. His family members were alive, in contact with him.

"My little brother was a famous NFL player," he said.

"Really? That's kind of cool. Shoot, I thought I was impressed my big sister was a high school and college basket-ball star. I'm such a klutz."

"Yeah, well, he retired, and he has a lot of money."

"You know what they say? You can't have too much money." Dana gave him her best smile, but it didn't do squat for his flat-line mouth. What a shame. He had a nice smile.

"Money didn't change my brother. He never was one for status objects."

"Sounds like a nice guy. Is he the one married to Talley?"

"The very one." His lips softened. "They make a great match. She's a tiger, and he's a softie. He'd do anything for her, for all of us."

"And the problem is...?"

Kyle huffed out a breath. "He wants to pay for things, like everything."

Good grief, how could that be bad? But something was

messing with Kyle, and she sensed he'd feel better once he shared it.

"I'm proud of my brother's success. But I don't want my little brother to buy me things. I'm not a charity case. My career path is longer, but I'm doing fine."

"Well, yeah. Surely your family doesn't question your success?"

"No. Of course not. But for now, it's better if I don't say anything."

For now? Was he insane? Tomorrow wasn't a guarantee. He was an oncologist, for heaven's sake. Every patient, every case presented an up-close-and-personal look at why people should live their best life every day.

CHAPTER NINE

K yle shifted to ease the bite to his backside from the patio chair. Duke University's fight song shattered the hum of conversations and birdsong in the overhead canopy. Talley again. Couldn't a guy enjoy lunch with an intriguing colleague? So much for his brilliant idea to attach the distinctive ringtone to Talley. Someday, he'd tell his sister-in-law where the tune came from.

Across from him, Dana wasn't laughing. Too bad. He liked her cute grin, especially when matched with the freckles sprinkled across her nose.

"That's her again, isn't it?"

"You win the prize." And he was definitely changing Talley's text tone.

"I love this lady. Tell me what she says." Her expressions were priceless. "Unless it's too personal."

These days, everything about his family was personal. But Dana was having too much fun to let it go. He tapped the screen. "I'd rather talk about Sam's next ball game."

"Thanks for the reminder. My daughter can be like a terrier with a bone." Dana slapped the heel of her hand against her forehead. "Speaking of dogs, she's begging for one of the neighbor's puppies. Anyway, she has a game Thursday evening and then another one on Tuesday, same time, same station. She wants you to come if you're free."

He'd make sure he was free. Attending last night's game had given him an energy boost.

He entered the game date and time into his calendar. "What kind of puppy?"

Duke's fight song cut through the silence, again.

"Some... kind of Yorkie mix." She tried unsuccessfully to stifle her giggles. "Talley seems to have a lot to say today. Come on, share. I used to love to read Robin's crazy texts. No matter how bad a day I was having, my big sister could make me laugh."

Now, he felt like a jerk, and the chocolate pudding had left an aftertaste. He'd be tasting the artificial flavor all day—just like he'd feel guilty all day if he read the text.

He'd sign with a practice soon and amass Whit's payment. He drained the last of his milk, but it didn't squelch the bitter taste in his mouth. The thought of crawling back to his family didn't help. He'd still be a jerk for letting Whit risk his life to finance his undergraduate education.

Besides, the last time he'd returned home for a Hope crisis, Talley blasted him with guilt. He had brothers and a stepfather, all capable men who could handle a Hope crisis. They didn't need him. He swiped the screen. "You've got to be kidding."

"Is it bad?"

Not bad, just surprising. "My little brother Nate is waffling between the Air Force and the Navy."

"Oh my goodness. I get this image of you in a uniform. Women will be all over him." She frowned. "Does Nate look like you?"

"He looks like Nate." He straightened. Did that mean she thought he'd look good in a uniform?

He shoved his glasses into place. If Dana continued the wide-eyed stare, her corneas would shrivel. What was with the eye thing anyway? Guys didn't do that, but Mom, Hope, Talley, and now Dana put it to use. No doubt, it was passed from mother to daughter. They probably perfected it in front of a mirror. Hope always claimed she was putting on makeup. Applying lipstick and eye stuff could not take an hour. They were practicing.

"Does he have dark hair and eyes?" Dana said.

He might as well go along with the conversation because she wasn't going to drop it. "We all do, except for Whit."

"Can people tell you're related?"

"Sure. Except with Whit's brown hair and blue eyes, he used to worry he was adopted. Murphy legend is we picked him up alongside the road."

"You did not tease a child with such a horrible story."

She was ticked? She'd asked the question.

"It was a joke," he said.

"Probably not to Whit."

Just what he needed, more guilt about his brother. He scrolled through Talley's latest. "Hope had a better day, but no telling how long that will last. My little sister has more ups and downs than an ECG—in V-tach."

"I bet there was never a moment of silence in the Murphy home." Her smile was contagious. "Sounds like fun."

"If you consider there was always a sibling to fight with as fun, the Murphy home meets the description."

"You also had confidants, someone to have your back, a person with shared history. That's important."

What the heck? He replayed the conversation. Two seconds ago, she was laughing, now she looked one breath away from tears.

"Look, my family is great. You're right, they've got my back. They're fun and caring people." But he didn't want to discuss them with Dana. "I just need some distance from them until I finish my fellowship and land a partnership."

"Never postpone contact," she said. "Trust me. I'd give everything I own for one more text from Robin or another hug from Mom."

When she put it that way— He raised his hands. "You're right. I'll text Talley this evening. I've got a difficult discussion with my patient in 612. Can you make time to attend it?"

Dana stood. "Since I don't agree with your aggressive treatments, that won't work for me. I'm here to support my patients' decisions, not persuade them to try new trials."

Kyle caught up with her. "I understand your perspective. I'm not asking you to compromise your principles. I just want you there to support her and help soften the information."

She dropped her trash in the receptacle. "Just so you understand, I'm not your yes-gal. If she asks for my opinion and I disagree, I'm giving it."

That could be trouble. Maybe this wasn't such a good idea. He could observe Dana without pulling her in on treatment options. He shook his head. If he wanted to expand his warm-fuzzy skills, he had to step up to the plate. Still...

"You're a good nurse and fabulous with people, but I've spent years studying the science. You don't want to intervene and give . . . misinformed information to a patient."

She shot him a narrow-eyed glare before jabbing the elevator button so hard it was a wonder her finger didn't go through the wall.

"Don't go postal on me." Since the elevator was vacant, he continued inside: "I spend hours at night going over new clinical data. What if you led a patient to make the wrong decision?"

"When it comes to the gut-wrenching decisions in cancer treatment, the patient and their family are always right."

"They don't—"

She jabbed her finger at him. "They know the physical, emotional, and spiritual needs of their family. You need to stifle your ego and listen."

"They hire me to guide them through the decisions."

"You are there to give them their options and the science behind the choices. You are *not* there to convince them of your opinion."

When the door slid open on 6-West, Dana marched off.

"Wait," he whispered. "Today, I'm just reviewing the treatment options."

Dana stopped, her blue eyes still narrowed in suspicion. "That's it?"

He nodded. "That's why I want your opinion. You can help me read Sarah's body language. Then maybe we can discuss—" He huffed out a breath. "And critique my presentation. I really do want to improve this component of my practice."

"On one condition."

Hallelujah, he'd gotten through to her. "Name your price." He couldn't believe he just said that. Knowing her, she'd want to remove part of his anatomy.

"You text Talley and show it to me—as long as it isn't personal."

"Are you—" He looked down the hall and lowered his voice. "Serious?"

"I'm as serious as glioblastoma. When I finish checking my patients, I'll accompany you to 612. After work, we can meet at the coffee shop right outside the hospital."

"Why are you focused on my family? You don't even know them."

"Because Talley sounds like a valiant warrior who knows

the importance of family. She needs a hand. If I can save one family from the pain of loss and regret I've suffered, I'm all in." She leaned closer. "Even when I have to counsel an arrogant man like you."

"I'm not arrogant. I'm good at my job."

"Me too!" Her nostrils flared, and her eyes narrowed.

His lip twitched, which was bizarre. Dana was overstepping her position in many ways. But the surprising notion of laughing quirked his mouth. Women. He'd never understand them.

Deal," he said. Although he felt compelled to enlist her help, the hairs at the back of his neck felt like they'd been rubbed the wrong direction.

"And—"

He shook his head. "There are no 'ands' in our agreement."

She crossed her arms. "Then the deal's off."

And he thought Talley and Hope rubbed him the wrong way. A room light clicked on across the hall.

"That's one of my patients."

"Dana? What are the additional terms?" he said through clenched teeth.

"You have to listen to my advice on family relationships."

"What? Now you're a family counselor? Things with my family are just fine."

She raised an eyebrow.

They were fine. Except he hadn't been home in over a year.

She had him in her crosshairs and knew it. How bad could it be? The memory of Talley's laughter accompanied the image of his sister-in-law. Whatever he agreed to, he'd better make sure Talley and Dana never got together.

"Okay," he said. He could live with the agreement for now. Besides, Dana always set her timer to thirty minutes. If he drew out the conversation on his patient, she wouldn't have time to harp on his family issues.

She checked her wristwatch. "I'll meet you in Sarah's room in thirty minutes."

The pudding aftertaste sharpened in his mouth. This deal was probably going to blow up in his face. Every time he was around Dana, something blew up—like his mind. He should've offered to take Sam on the bike ride. After dealing with the kid's mother, he could use more downtime.

CHAPTER TEN

D ana gripped the heavy room door but didn't slam it in Kyle's face. He wasn't the problem; she was. His family issues were none of her business. Kyle was a friend. She helped friends. What if a friend had advised her to make family a priority before the accident? What if she'd been told to savor the extra hug, say I love you?

Except Kyle didn't act receptive to her advice. He was a good guy with a caring family. If she could help them, she needed to do it. That was another thing. Why did everything have to be a barter with him? Competitions required a winner and a loser. With Robin, Dana always lost, which resulted in an unnecessary emphasis on rivalry.

In the end, Dana had lost her sister. Maybe if she'd been more focused on her relationship with Robin instead of competing with her, the guilt wouldn't cut as sharp.

Thirty-three minutes later, Dana met Kyle outside Room 612. Although she'd cared for other patients with pancreatic cancer, read about cutting-edge treatments, seen the advertisements, she wanted to weep for Sarah Gates and her family. Kyle's options held little hope and a lot of misery.

Worse, Kyle's turned-down mouth and shuddered gaze mirrored the despair weighting her feet. Dana squared her shoulders; her sadness wouldn't help her patient. If Sarah could face her fate, Dana would support and witness her courage. What she couldn't do was get on board with Kyle if her patient didn't agree with aggressive therapy.

When they entered Sarah's room, a gardenia-scented body lotion replaced the hospital sanitizer. Seated in the only two chairs at the foot of the bed, Sarah and her husband Mike waited. Kyle sat on the end of the bed, facing the couple, while Dana remained standing at his side. With Sarah's hand gripped in his, Mike appeared cornered and fiercely protective of his wife. From the look of Sarah's sad features, she'd already lost hope. Nursing had been Dana's passion since her first day volunteering. Today, she'd prefer cleanup duty behind the zoo elephants.

Kyle had rearranged his features behind an unwavering determination—except for his facial tic. She'd first spied the twitch in his cheek when he notified Mrs. Kramer of her husband's death. Sam displayed a similar twitch when Dana prepared unfamiliar foods. Kyle must anticipate a distasteful discussion.

Unlike earlier rapid-fire explanations, Kyle softened and lowered his voice. His words sliced through the air, presenting a positive outlook of the latest treatments. He shared handouts with Mike and Sarah and suggested they study them later.

Although he incorporated the advice they talked about, that didn't change Sarah's grim prognosis. If Dana hadn't reviewed the literature, she might have rallied some hope. She didn't. Mike sat stone-still, his hand clasping his wife's, and his gaze distant. Sarah's affect remained flat, lifeless.

Kyle stood and then halted. "Can I answer questions for you?"

Dana cleared her throat, but Kyle didn't return to his seat. Didn't he understand? He could answer treatment questions and provide statistics, but not *why* Sarah had developed the disease. He couldn't give advice on, or how to tell their children their mother was dying, or about watching their hopes and their dreams disappear.

Kyle shoved his hands in his pockets. "I realize this is—"

"Here at Wilcox, we practice a team approach." Dana sidestepped Kyle and knelt at Sara's feet. "Dr. Murphy has explained the science. Now, it's my turn. This is a lot of complex information to process." She glanced over her shoulder giving Kyle a nonverbal cue to follow her lead. Right now, he looked about as stunned as her patient—just for a different reason.

From her pocket, she removed a notepad with a cheery design on the cover and matching pen. "Since you're stable, I believe Dr. Murphy plans to discharge you. That will give you time to go home, relax in a safe space."

When Kyle stepped closer, she glanced his way. A scowl wrinkled his forehead, and his lips had thinned.

She turned back to Sarah. "On the inside cover, I've written my contact information. To improve your remission chances, we need to minimize stress, which can be triggered by the unknown. Once you get home and rest, questions will surface. Please contact me any time you have an urgent question. For all other concerns, questions, even if they seem trivial or inconsequential, document them in your notebook. Text me, and we'll set up a time to talk. If I can answer your questions, I will. If they're more technical, I'll confer with Dr. Murphy. We meet every day to discuss our patients."

"Thanks," Sarah whispered.

Dana stood and faced Kyle. His scowl had deepened, but his lips were pressed into a grim line. He wasn't going to lose his mind in front of his patients. No doubt, he'd lose it with her at the coffeehouse. Perhaps she'd suggest a walk. Or, better yet, a run. Based on the frequency of his tic, he needed a release.

"I'd like to see you in the clinic tomorrow—"

"They'll need at least two days," Dana said.

Although she'd turned her back on Kyle, the heat of his stare warmed her backside. Oblivious to their professional conflict, Sarah stared at the notebook in her hands, but Mike made eye contact.

Tears moistened his eyes. "Make it next Monday. I'd like to take my wife to the beach for the weekend. My parents are watching the kids."

"Monday it is," Dana said, ignoring the grunt from Kyle.

Oh boy, she'd probably overstepped on that one. But Kyle would get over it. Mike and Sarah couldn't. They needed every moment they could scratch out of their remaining life together.

"Remember, there's no bad question," Dana said. "If none are urgent, bring them with you to review with Dr. Murphy."

While Kyle went over discharge instructions, she exited to finish up her shift. Maybe she'd run late and bow out of the coffeehouse meetup.

Forty minutes later, after making her final patient check, Dana walked to the unit desk to report off.

Kyle stopped her. "We need to talk."

His rough tone accelerated her heart rate, but she remained calm. "At the coffeehouse, as we agreed."

"No—"

"Sorry." She tapped her watch. "If I don't finish up, I'll be staying overtime, and I won't be able to meet." She gave him a finger wave. "See you at four."

Despite the slack in his jaw—he really did have sexy scruff —she had work to do, and he might need a few minutes to breathe.

Although today would have been the perfect day to run late, Dana finished her shift on time. Kyle entered the quaint coffee shop five minutes after she'd placed her order and selected a two-top table beneath the outside awning. Too bad they didn't have giant booths or even a picnic table. No doubt, distance from Kyle might be a good thing for their meeting. But she had a plan.

He sat across from her, his dark eyebrows merging over his narrow glasses.

"Beautiful afternoon," she said. "This banana bread is divine. I can share."

"I'm not hungry."

She pasted a pleasant expression on her face. If she put out negative thoughts, she'd receive negative results. He'd asked for her help, but her patients took priority. She'd done her best. This time, however, her best hadn't been great for Kyle.

The dense cake tasted like cardboard. "Mmm. I really don't need the additional calories, but what's that saying? 'Life's short. Eat dessert first.'"

His lips didn't move.

"I think it's a good motto." She broke off another bite and choked it down with a stiff smile. "Have you responded to your sister-in-law?"

He narrowed his eyes.

"I'll take that as a no."

"You were out of line." The firm set to his mouth and jaw were so tight his lips were the only thing that moved.

He was apparently out of patience. Dana huffed out a breath. She loved banana bread, but not when she had to choke it down. Not when she'd delayed the conversation for as long as she could.

"Very well. Let's start with a critique of your delivery." She leaned forward and met his steely gaze. "Know your audience.

Sarah and Mike couldn't hear a word you said after your opening line with her diagnosis. When you see your patient's eyes glaze over, close your mouth and open your heart and ears."

"They came to me to diagnose Sarah's disease and manage treatment options."

"True, but timing is everything. Immediately after you give a grim diagnosis is not always the time. It wasn't the time with Mike and Sarah." And her harsh delivery wasn't much better than his. But he was very stubborn.

"Draw on your experience with Mr. Harris." She softened her voice. "You're very good with the science, but you forgot to consider your patient and her husband's perspective."

He raked long fingers through his hair, causing the strands to stick out at odd angles. "There's not a lot of hope if she doesn't start treatment soon."

"From what I've read, there's a poor prognosis regardless of treatment initiation."

"But it's up to me to find an option. Find some hope for her and her family."

"You asked for a decision, and they couldn't think. They needed time, compassion. The only plus on your execution was the handouts. Tomorrow or the next day, Sarah and Mike might be able to review and comprehend them."

Although his gaze had softened, she was uncertain if he had hit listening mode. She wasn't perfect and she'd made mistakes reading nonverbal cues. But she was pretty sure about Kyle, which was odd. Her past relationships with men ranked below his delivery skills. Ha! He'd probably enjoy the tidbit.

"The sooner we treat the disease, the better her chances for remission."

"One weekend together isn't going to change Sarah's outcome."

He blinked, then moistened his lips. She had him there. Dana nipped the inside of her cheek to maintain her neutral expression. He was listening now. She'd worked diligently to improve her nonverbal assessment cues. Reading body language became imperative in oncology. She couldn't help others if she didn't practice listening and awareness. Although she'd practiced on other healthcare professionals, she hadn't applied those skills to Kyle. How was he different than the score of physicians who marched through their unit?

She tore off the bent corner of her napkin. This was no time to change her process, which would be unfair to him and unwise for her.

"The notebook." His cheek twitched with the tic she'd seen before. "It's a good idea. But I'd like my patients to contact me."

"Give me some business cards, and I'll add them to my stash. I buy the notebooks whenever they go on sale, so I always have a supply."

He removed his phone from his pocket and typed on the screen. "I'll get some made."

She could be wrong, but something about his expression had changed. "Anything else?"

"I always analyze the conversations I have with patients. What did I learn? What can I add for the next time I talk with a patient?"

He broke off a piece of her banana bread and popped it into his mouth. The movement of his full upper lip clouded her thoughts. She blinked.

"A weekend away," he was saying.

"Sorry. I missed your last thought." No doubt, he wouldn't miss the embarrassing blush heating her cheeks.

"I could suggest my patients take a weekend off to get away and talk, especially couples with kids at home. Hospital rooms have improved over the years, but they still aren't the best environment for life choices."

"Exactly." Dana picked up crumbs with her index finger but didn't eat them.

"You should've checked with me about the discharge."

"You're right." She nodded. "But we're just starting this team. It takes time to hammer out the wrinkles."

His cheek twitched again. What emotion did it signal? Her bet? It was more than one.

"Are you sure I can't buy you a piece of bread?"

He shook his head.

"Fine. Let me see your text to Talley."

His expression hardened. Clearly, his family issues were deep-seated.

"You know, people can be foolish." She raised her hand. "Me included. I used to let trivial things wiggle between me and my loved ones. But after Mom and Robin—" She swallowed. Even after over a year, it was sometimes hard to talk about them. Which validated her point. She squared her shoulders. "Losing them unexpectedly forced me to filter out the insignificant stuff."

"That's got to be tough."

"So, what's the issue with your family?"

"There is no issue. Talley sent an invitation to a baby shower."

Dana snapped her slackened jaw closed. "A baby? OMG, that's exciting. Is this the first time for you as an uncle?"

"Yes."

"So, of course, you're going. Is she having a girl or a boy? You are going to fall in love with this niece or nephew. They are fun, especially toddlers. By that time, you'll be finished with your fellowship and have more time to spend with the baby."

"Talley is having a girl."

"OMG, they have the cutest baby clothes for little girls. The boy things are cute too, but finding them can be a challenge. But the bonnets and little dresses and boots. I love boots on toddlers."

"Perfect. You can pick out the gift to send."

Dana snapped her mouth closed. Now, who had the listening problem? She softened her tone. "You won't need to send anything if you attend the shower."

"I'm not going to a baby shower. I'll visit after my niece arrives."

"No wonder you have family issues." *Hush, Dana. You're in preacher mode.* She forced a smile. "The shower is a celebration for your very first niece. You can't blow it off."

"I'm not blowing it off. I'll send a dress—with boots." He dug in his pocket and pulled out his wallet. "How much do you think it will cost? You can't go wild. I'm still paying off loans and saving for a practice. Some practices let you buy in right away."

"You should attend the shower. If for no other reason than to support your brother. I'm sure Talley has lots of friends."

"I can't take time off."

"Of course you can. We don't work twenty-four seven."

"Talley and Whit live in Sunberry." Kyle withdrew two twenty-dollar bills. "It's over two hours from here."

Dana wiggled her fingers. "Let me see the text."

Kyle shrugged, tapped in the password, and shoved the phone her way. The minute she started typing, he placed a warm palm over her hand. Tingles ran across her wrist.

"I agreed to advice only," he said, not moving his hand.

She had to admit the connection was...nice. Although she couldn't remember admiring a man's hand, other than to access a vein, Kyle's long fingers and olive-skinned wrists were—

Dana swallowed. Were they having a moment?

The bell above the coffee shop door tinkled, and the aroma of coffee and sugar whirled around her with the faint breeze. Muted voices disappeared. A car hummed beside them on the road.

He was probably staring at her, and he still hadn't removed his hand.

She looked up. His straight nose and long chin kept him from being Hollywood gorgeous. But he could hold his own in the looks department. He sure was holding her.

"Unless we're working a double, we're meeting here after work?" The low timbre of his voice, as gentle as his touch, stroked her ears.

He was probably a good kisser. She straightened in the chair. Oh, that would work, just peachy. The Wilcox Memorial grapevine would hum over the single oncology fellow and oncology nurse making out at the coffee shop. She fanned her face with her hand. Man, it was hot for April.

When he released her, air whistled through her teeth. Had she been holding her breath?

"Works for me." Her voice had an odd vibration to it. Drat, the man.

"I need more than thirty minutes. When's your next extra shift?"

"Tomorrow. But Paula hired two new grads for the evening shift. I may not get a regular break."

"What's that, nine for you?"

Dana nodded. While she was on the final countdown, he had stalled. She hid a smile. Although she'd resented competition with her sister, her banter with Kyle made working the extra shifts a little more palatable.

"It's only 4:28."

She tucked her hand beneath the table, away from the lure of him. She'd promised Sam, and Sam remained her priority. "Sorry, Dr. Murphy. I have a standing date with Sam."

"She's a great kid."

"Your new niece will be a great kid too." She pointed at his phone still perched between them. "Text Talley and tell her you're coming to the shower."

"Compromise." He tapped the screen. "I'll text her I can't make it."

After a flurry of taps, he slid his phone to her.

KYLE: Thanks for the invitation but gotta work that day.

DANA LOOKED UP AT HIM. "Really? That's the best you've got?"

"Picky, picky, picky." Kyle swiped the screen. "I'll just use the decline I used for the St. Patrick's Day party." He swiped again.

"Let me guess, you didn't decline and didn't show."

"Come on. It was a St. Patty's Day party. I meant to. Something at the hospital probably distracted me." He thumbed faster. "I had a nice line for New Year's. Maybe it was Christmas."

"You've never responded to any of them?" At least he looked embarrassed. She pressed her fingers against his to stop his scrolling. He wasn't going to find anything. "That's sad. You have, what, two brothers and a sister, plus your parents, and you don't join them for family celebrations?" Tears stung her eyes. "You don't even answer them."

"I just did." He closed the app and slid the phone into his pocket. "Advice received. Tomorrow lunch and dinner break?"

This was a mistake. She couldn't enlighten the unenlightened. Kyle inhabited a cave—a lightless one. Wasn't that the way of life? She'd found an attractive man who was a compassionate physician and good with kids. She'd considered moving forward, and then bam! A man who held his family in such low regard wasn't for her.

"But you've still got two extra shifts on me." Kyle was looking at his phone calendar. "I'm filling in for Craig. It's his wife's birthday. However..." He jabbed at his phone. "There's a need for a second physician from 6:00 P.M. until midnight. A six-hour shift counts, right?"

She clamped her jaw shut at the irony. For such a smart man, Kyle could be very obtuse. However, further commentary on her part was useless.

"That will bring me to trailing by one," he said. "I'll be in the clinic tomorrow. I'll text you around lunchtime."

Maybe it was time he was on the receiving end of his unresponsiveness. Dana tossed her trash in the receptacle and walked toward the parking garage. Her daughter's smile would lighten her day. Sam lit up her life, and she planned to ensure her little angel knew that. Kyle's voice called out behind her, but she didn't turn. He wasn't for her. He'd get the hint once she stopped meeting him during her breaks.

A breeze lifted her hair. The mild afternoon was perfect for a bike ride with her special girl. And she'd ensure Sam never forgot the meaning of family ties.

CHAPTER ELEVEN

While Dana made her getaway toward the parking garage, Kyle unlocked his bike. Was it something he said, or was she trying to honor her promise to her daughter? Two women passed him on the wide sidewalk, their eyes narrowed on him. He glanced around. What? Did he have "bad boy" blinking on his forehead? Just because a man appreciated the swing of a curvy woman's hips didn't mean he was a perv. It meant he was interested, and Dana continued to interest him.

Swinging his leg over the seat, Kyle shoved off. Sam and Dana would enjoy a bike ride, especially on a perfect day. It was too nice to spend the evening indoors. Minor problem. Dana hadn't invited him. She'd acted like he'd developed a serious disease.

Considering she'd been insubordinate in front of his patient, he thought he'd been calm. Some physicians might have reprimanded a junior colleague. Although he'd been angry, he'd accepted her advice. Business cards were a no-brainer. He should've thought of them. And the notebook idea? He picked up the pace. Just like Dana, a notebook was straightforward and effective.

At the crosswalk, he slowed and then pedaled harder toward the Wilcox entry. That was the thing about her. What you saw is what you got. She didn't go for the games many of his previous dates employed. Some women acted as though a physician were a piece of meat. Men had feelings too, and he was starting to get this touchy-feely thing. He just needed to stop every now and then and check in to his patients' expressions. That was the key. Thank you, Dana Graham. His gratitude would put a smile on her face.

At the hospital bike rack, he waited for a staffer to pull a bike from a slot. Dana hadn't smiled this afternoon. For a moment, she looked like she might cry. But that was crazy. Why would she cry about his interactions with his family?

His cheek kept twitching. The stupid tic could be as annoying as relationships. His life was super busy right now, and with the finish line in sight, he couldn't let a baby shower blow up his plan. He also didn't want to blow up his chance with Dana. She was making him a better physician. He'd need an edge with his new partners. Speaking of partners, he should have heard from Triangle Oncology by now. They were probably busy too.

The following night, Kyle shivered in his light jacket and leaned against the garage support. The temperature continued to drop, and the damp concrete garage did nothing to retain warmth. Across from him, Dana's Corolla sat adjacent to the elevator beneath a garage light. She'd supposedly been too busy to take a lunch break, but she also canceled their dinner meeting. Unexpected events happened on a unit, but two in a row? She was avoiding him, which didn't make sense. Sure, he didn't attract women like Whit and his football groupies, but he didn't scare them away. Not that he was looking to date Dana. At least not *yet*.

He checked the time. She should be here soon, especially since she wasn't scheduled to meet him. No way would he ask her to go on a picnic after she'd blown him off for lunch and dinner in the stinking hospital cafeteria. He just wanted to know why.

What happened to her agreement to help him improve patient awareness? Kyle rolled his shoulders. At least it sounded better than expanding his touchy-feely perspective. Who said things like that out loud? He was a small-town guy from Sunberry, North Carolina, not some progressive man.

This time she wasn't going to avoid him. If he'd screwed up, he'd own it. He didn't like the thought, but he was man enough to meet his mistakes head-on—even those with his brother. Tonight, he'd finished one more shift toward his heart-to-heart with Whit.

When the elevator dinged, he straightened. The door slid open, and Dana, alone in the elevator car, hesitated, her eyes wide. After a pause she moved forward fast and purposeful. He could almost hear the argument rolling behind those stunning eyes.

"I'm really tired." She pointed her key fob at the Corolla, and a hushed click filled the silence in the garage.

"Me too—of your excuses." He folded his arms across his chest. "Mind telling me what's going on?"

She opened the car door and pitched her lunch bag and purse onto the passenger seat. For a moment, he thought she was going to get inside and drive off without talking to him.

After closing the door, she turned to face him. "I think you got the wrong idea about—"

"I'm not buying it. I may need more practice on my awareness, but not about you."

She glanced away. "That wasn't our agreement."

He moved closer. She'd taught him about subtle hints, and

he couldn't chance missing one. Not tonight. "I want to change the agreement."

"I want to end it," she said.

His arms fell to his sides. What the heck had happened? Before he could come up with a response, she glanced away. Was that a waiver?

Go for it. At this point, he had little to lose. Murphys never gave up, even when the circumstances looked futile.

"I need your help." His admission was harder to hear than to say. "I can be a jerk. I don't work at it or anything."

His cheek spasmed. "There's just a lot to focus on. The worse thing I can do is make the wrong decision. Screw up or miss a diagnosis. Do you know how many times I review the data, test results, my exam?"

"My decision isn't based on your skill set."

"No, it's based on my limitations. Which makes it more important for you to help me. Plus, I suck at picking out baby clothes."

She blinked, made eye contact. Finally, he was getting through to her. He'd run through his memory tape of yesterday's conversation so many times that his head nearly blew off. What the heck had he said to set her against him? Not just a little, but a lot.

"I want to send something... Man, this sounded dumb. "Something special. I spent hours on the Internet last night. Did you know they have infant cheerleader clothes? Not that Talley or Whit will want them. Whit retired. He doesn't need a reminder. Plus, Talley's kind of a feminist. She wouldn't be thrilled if I sent something like that to her daughter."

How the heck was a guy supposed to figure out so many expressions? Man, he was just learning this skill. Dana could contort her facial features into more looks than Talley and Hope combined.

Kyle pulled at his collar. "Have you ever heard of an online store called Itsy? Maybe that's not it."

"Etsy."

He suppressed the urge to pump his fist. Her code of silence was making him crazy. "That's probably it. I found this ballerina-like outfit. You know, with the ruffly stuff at the hips? Anyway, it says, 'My Uncle Loves Me.' It's purple and white with sparkly gold writing, and it has this headband-like thing with this big gold bow." He couldn't believe the words that were coming out of his mouth. He sounded like an idiot. Talley would hate a gold bow. "Oh, and it's a one-something with snaps in the crotch. I guess that makes it easier to change diapers."

At least she was grinning now. Probably because she thought he sounded as much a fool as he did. If his brothers heard this conversation, he'd be toast. Funny, he almost wished they did. He'd missed their ribbing.

"Kyle?"

He straightened. "Don't get offended. It's not personal, just the way I'm wired. My brain will zone out with a random triggered thought. I was thinking about how my brothers would respond to the baby-clothes description. Our big pastime was calling each other out. Nate, man, he was good. He has a wit like a knife. Whit has this great laugh because you know it comes straight from his heart. He's not big on sarcasm. At least, not like me and Nate."

"You miss them," she said.

What? He blinked. "I forgot the point I was making."

"I said you miss them."

Something had changed her mind because the frown lines in her forehead had smoothed. His fingers itched to push back her hair. She'd have soft skin. This was the Dana who haunted his dreams.

Ah, man. He needed to stop thinking, especially about kissing her. "Can I?"

She canted her chin to the right, and shadows danced along her cheek. Her gaze lowered. When he ran his hand along her neck, she leaned closer.

"Are you thinking about kissing me?"

"Perceptive."

Her slim fingers fanned against his chest. "Chop-chop, before I change my mind."

It was a little awkward kissing and smiling. Her lips moved against his, warm and sweet. *Never manhandle a woman*, Mom had cautioned, but his hands were already pressing her hips closer. When she exhaled, he pressed his advantage and deepened the kiss.

Why couldn't he be a swimmer with a huge lung capacity? Reluctantly, he released her lips, but not her hips. He could breathe just fine with his hands cradling her firm backside. An image of what she might look like without her uniform flashed in his mind.

"Kyle," she whispered.

He kissed the silky skin beneath her ear. She shivered.

"Kyle." This time she was more insistent.

"Right here, where I want to be," he said.

"Well, we're also in a public parking garage."

"You could come to my apartment." He nuzzled her neck, savoring her scent. "I don't have anything stronger than milk, but I have peanut butter."

"Dad stays with Sam when I work evenings."

"You're killing me, Dana Graham. In so many ways."

"I was trying to put some distance between us."

"Why? We're great together. Not just your help with my awareness, but us. I understand you must be careful about Sam, but I'm all in. I'd like to take the next step, take you out, see where this goes."

When she stared at his shoes, he tensed. She wanted him. He might be behind at this awareness thing, but a man knew when a woman was receptive. And her kiss? She was in, except for something holding her back.

"I can't be with a man who disregards his family."

"Disregards?" What the heck?

"Sorry," she whispered. "This won't work for me."

"Wait! I agree I've been a jerk. But it's not disregard. I mean, I love all of them. They're great—most of the time. Hope is a teenager and being a huge thorn in the side for everyone. But she'll figure it out. At least that's the Murphy hope." He chuckled.

Dana didn't.

"You don't have the whole picture. You know my brother was a Carolina Cougar, right? She nodded.

"Whit's this super nice guy. He fits the saying about giving the shirt from his back. But I can't let him do it anymore. I'm only eleven shifts from fixing this. My fellowship will be over, and I'll hopefully have a partnership. I'll be my own man. After that, Whit won't feel compelled or obligated..." Kyle shook his hands. "Who knows the reason? I just know I can't let him pay my way."

"So you avoid the family?"

"No. Not really."

Ah, jeez. A single raised brow. Even a caveman could understand the expression. "I know it looks... But if anyone needs something, I'm there. They know that."

She crossed her arms in front of her chest. "Because you're such a great communicator?"

"I'll be sure to introduce you to my family. You'd fit right in with the comebacks."

"You know this isn't right." Dana opened the car door. "It's your family and your business. But I'd give a year's salary to be with my family again. Family is a rare gift. And you ignore yours. Sorry, but that's sad. So, too bad, if it's unwanted advice or nagging or whatever you consider my butting into your life."

Yes, it was unwanted advice, but at least she was back to the Dana he knew. "Wait."

She was already in the car, reaching for her seat belt. Kyle stepped between the open door and kneeled to be level with her.

"You don't owe me an explanation," she said, her features sad but resolved.

For some reason, this was a deal-breaker for her, and he wasn't prepared to let her break the connection between them.

"I like my family. They like me. This...what you're witnessing...it's temporary. Eleven more shifts and it goes away."

"I'm happy for you, really. But I've got to get home. Dad is probably starting to worry."

"Tomorrow, lunch?" He dipped his chin to watch her features. "I really need advice on a baby gift."

She was giving in. He could feel it. Although something was still messing with her, she was giving him another chance. All he needed was more time. He'd show her he wasn't a threat to her daughter. Man, he'd put on kid gloves for her.

"I'm off tomorrow."

Don't push. Get back on an even keel before asking her for a date or a picnic. "Friday?"

"Families are priority for me, but I'll think about it." The car's shadowed interior emphasized the intensity of her gaze.

They were for him too. It was just a difference in perspective. He nodded, but his cheek twitched to the beat of his heart.

CHAPTER TWELVE

At the garage exit, Dana dropped her forehead against the cool padded steering wheel. She should've made a clean break. Why did she leave it open with him? Because it was the right thing to do. She needed to help others.

Life wasn't just about her wants and fears. It was about contribution, about improving another's life. Most of the time she helped patients. This time, she needed to help Kyle and his family. Although she hadn't planned to, hadn't wanted to, she cared about Kyle. He was a good man, and he dedicated his life to helping others. All he'd asked was for her help to make him a better physician. But he had a more urgent need and didn't realize it.

When a shiver raced over her shoulders, she adjusted the heat and wheeled onto the road home. How would Kyle bear the guilt if something happened to a family member, to the baby? She had to help him remove the blinders. Her help, however, didn't require kissing him.

The streetlights illuminated the car's interior in rhythmic shadows. The memory of his leather scent tingled along her limbs. She turned off the heat and lowered the window. Air brushed past her lips like a kiss. He'd been gentle, almost tentative, until she'd almost devoured him. She squeezed the steering wheel as the Corolla bumped over the curb to her cottage.

"Help him with his family, not his kissing."

He clearly didn't need assistance with the latter. However, if she wanted to help him, she'd need to know why he avoided his family. Since his family members were reaching out, he was the stodgy part. Her bet, forgiveness festered at the heart of the matter. Something had happened. Something he hadn't managed to work through. Managing guilt still challenged her.

Her headlights swung across the front of her cottage. She'd put another shift under her belt.

"Almost there, Mom. Nine more shifts, and I'll have the down payment on my own home."

Even Robin would be proud. For that reason, she understood Kyle's motivation to establish his own practice, even admired his ambition. The creak of the car door interrupted her thoughts. Helping Kyle was a noble goal, but her help couldn't put Sam at risk.

She'd always dreamed of a big loving family, not a big, estranged family. Worse, she'd not only agreed to continue meeting with him, but she'd also kissed him. Was she making the decision to go forward with Kyle based on her hormones or her head? It for sure wasn't based on her heart because she'd only known him, really known him, for a short while. Working side by side as physician and nurse didn't count.

She sucked in a breath and locked her car. Thank goodness she had a day off, away from his handsome influence to figure out her next move.

After catching up on household chores the following day, Dana navigated the long hall decorated with stick figures, handprints, and rainbows to Sam's preschool class.

"Mommy!" Sam raced to her and wrapped her arms around her neck.

Twenty-four hours is a long time, Kyle Murphy. And he'd gone months. "Hey, munchkin. Did you leave room for ice cream? I went to the store this morning."

"Strawberry?" Sam skipped to the car. "Joey's dad bought him a ferret."

She fastened the seat belt over Sam's booster seat. "I missed you too. Do you think I could get another hug?"

She was expecting open arms, not rodent news. Were ferrets considered rodents? No doubt, her daughter would have the details.

Sam complied—for all of two seconds. "He named it Smokey, and it likes to cuddle around his neck. Since I don't have a daddy, can *you* get me a ferret?"

Dana closed the car door, wishing she could close the door on the conversation. But her little one had picked up her persistence trait. "Pets are a big responsibility."

Like children. Except children had an uncanny knack for strumming the guilt strings. Sam didn't have a dad because of Dana's bad decisions, and she wasn't getting a ferret because—

The Corolla's engine hummed to life. Because Dana knew nothing about ferrets. Her luck they'd make a mistake, and the animal would die.

A shudder slinked down her spine. Sam had suffered enough losses for one little girl. No way would Dana set her up for another.

"Joey feeds Smokey from his hand. He said his whiskers tickle."

She turned into their drive.

"I'm ticklish." Sam peeked over the console the moment the engine switched off.

"Pets need food and water all the time. They need exercise and a clean cage."

"I can do those things." Instead of darting to the house, Sam stayed one inch from her elbow until she stopped inside at the small dinette set. She dropped her book bag on the floor. "Can we get a ferret?"

Dana removed the ice cream from the freezer. "If you show me you can be responsible, we'll talk when you turn six."

"That's a long time."

Although Sam remained silent while she dished out ice cream, the wheels inside her daughter's mind were almost visible.

She slid the ice cream in front of Sam and kissed her tousled head. "Time goes by faster than you think. It seems like yesterday I was bringing you home from the hospital. You were my little gift."

"I like presents. I want a ferret present."

Of course she did. While Sam devoured her snack, Dana explained the difference between talk and action. She paused halfway through the explanation. Kyle and Sam were in the same category on that one. He said he would respond to his sister-in-law, but he put it off until she'd checked. Great, helping Kyle was like acquiring another child.

After setting up a Good Girl Sticker Award system for Sam to show the girl could care for a pet, Dana was ready with ideas for Kyle on Friday.

At two o'clock Friday afternoon, Dana's cell alerted. She checked her patient's IV, then stepped inside the utility room to view her text.

KYLE: Change of plans. 30-minute road trip. Pick you up in front of coffee shop. Green Subaru.

. . .

DANA CLEARED THE SCREEN. Road trip? Kyle rode his bike to work. Apparently not today. She hadn't agreed to a road trip, and how far did he think he could travel in her thirty-minute window? Time to set more limits.

At three-forty-five Dana crossed the street to the coffee house. Except for two motorcycles parked adjacent to the building, the street remained vacant. When she turned her wrist to check the time, a horn sounded behind her. Kyle waved through the windshield.

Dana slid into the passenger seat. "Where are you taking me?"

Kyle shifted. "Hillsborough. A group there contacted me." He glanced at her, his glasses working down the bridge of his nose. "I just want to drive by the office and get a feel for the town."

"I thought you wanted to partner with Triangle?"

"I do. I'm just checking my options." He hit his blinker to turn. "I like Triangle's proximity to the hospital network, but the traffic is a pain."

"Burdens and benefits," Dana said. "I like small towns. But Wilcox was hiring new graduates, and I needed a job."

"You'd like Sunberry. It's a perfect size. Small enough to know your neighbors and large enough for nice amenities."

So why didn't he move back?

He shook his head like he was carrying on an inner dialogue. "When Mom first moved us there from Charlotte, I hated it."

"How old were you?"

"Fifteen."

"Teen years are a challenge. At that age, nothing seems to fit right."

"I was in an angry phase," he said. "I also thought I was in charge. You know, the take-charge fifteen-year-old trying to be the man of the house."

An image of a young Kyle, trying to be a man for his mom, created a lump in her throat. "Paula swears it's in the DNA for boys to care for their single moms."

"Pretty much. Anyway, Sunberry was just what I needed. I would've gone down the wrong road if Mom had stayed in Charlotte."

"I like that about small towns. In Blowing Rock, we knew everyone. Here, I don't know the families. Sam came home yesterday wanting a ferret. It would be nice to know the child's mother, so I could get the inside scoop."

He shot her a knowing smile. "Like how often she cleans the cage?"

Leave it to Kyle to make her laugh. "The surgical resident's cat had a new litter of kittens. They're part Nebelung. It's a fancy cat breed. Anyway, they're known for their beautiful coats." Kyle slowed outside of an older building renovated into an oncology office. "Not bad. It's got a homey vibe."

But there was something about the way he spoke. "Not what you envisioned?" she said.

"I like the convenience of a nearby hospital."

Dana glanced at him. She'd never seen him undecided about anything, unless— "Does Sunberry have a hospital?"

He sped up and turned toward the center of town. "A hospital, a small college, and an opera house."

"Wow! It does sound perfect."

"It's a nice place—to visit."

"Sounds like a nice place to raise a family. I can see why your mom moved there. I love living close to work." She checked the time. "Speaking of—"

He lifted his thumb. "On it. Bike ride with Sam tonight?"

"Yep."

"What's the latest from Talley?" The Subaru sped along the highway. He wasn't going to wiggle out of their deal this time.

"I met my part of the agreement," she said, smiling to soften the sharpness in her voice.

When he frowned, his dark brows merged with the tops of his glasses, creating a dark expression. "We haven't talked about patients. Any news from Sarah?"

"No. But just because we don't have a current patient issue doesn't mean you're off the hook on the family side."

"Is it okay if I just enjoy being with you?" He stared straight ahead, his knuckles white from his grip on the steering wheel.

"I wouldn't be here if I didn't enjoy your company."

That was the problem. She was starting to enjoy it too much. Although she looked forward to the patient discussions and learning new insights in medicine, she and Kyle... fit. With him, she'd found acceptance, respect, laughter. She swallowed. And desire. Conversation between them flowed regardless if they discussed medicine, sports, children, or life.

But if there was going to be a 'them,' he had to resolve his family issues. And if he didn't? Could she walk away? What if something happened? She'd never be able to forgive herself, and she couldn't knowingly let him suffer. The night Dad had called, broken and sobbing, clawed at her mind. Kyle would lose loved ones in his life. She couldn't protect him from loss. But she could help him be more mindful of his loved ones now.

And the stinker was resisting again. "So something is clearly up with Talley or someone else in the family."

"She threatened me," he said in a burst of words.

Dana blinked. "How does that work? A pregnant woman who lives over two hours away is a threat to, what, a six-foot man?"

"Five feet eleven."

"Wow! A shrimp under the six-foot mark."

His sexy mouth remained grim, and if he gripped the steering wheel any tighter, it might crumble.

He glanced at her, his features set in a scowl. "She's threatening to move the shower to Raleigh, so I can attend."

Dana slapped her hand over her mouth until she had her giggle under control, deepening his scowl. "I'm sorry, but—" She raised her palms. "I really need to meet this Talley. OMG, she's amazing."

"Relocating the shower is not amazing. It's ridiculous. Plus, she wouldn't just move the location to Raleigh; she'd move up the date. I'm sure Mom and Grandma Stella have been working for weeks to set this up. I'm not going to be responsible for making the entire family take a road trip and spoiling their plans."

It was illogical and sweet. "Sounds like it's important you attend."

"I told her I was busy Saturday."

She waved her hand. "Remember me? I'm the gal who has an ongoing competition with you to meet the OT goals. You" —she pointed at him— "are not working next weekend. It's Spring Fling."

"I volunteered for the dunking pool."

"You did not. You told me you'd never agree to dunking torture."

"Paula can be very convincing."

"Paula is my BFF. She was dying to have you on the roster because she thought you'd draw a big crowd and lots of money. If you had agreed, I'd know it by now."

"I decided last night. I just haven't had time to tell Paula."

Unbelievable. "I can see why you don't want them to move the shower to Raleigh. But why put you and your family through unnecessary grief? Just tell them you'll come to Sunberry."

He kept his gaze on the road, which was not a good sign.

"So what did you tell Talley?" she pressed.

"I told you I'd start responding. I have."

Right, and she'd bet her next shift he hadn't responded yet. She needed to start a Good Boy Sticker Award poster for him and gift it to him. When a snicker slipped from her lips, he shot her a fierce glare.

She held out her hand. "According to our agreement, you have to share your response with me."

"Here we are." He pulled to the curb adjacent to the hospital parking garage. "Twenty-nine minutes. Thanks, Kyle," he mimicked her. "You are prompt."

She returned her nastiest glare.

He smiled. "We can continue tomorrow at lunch. Are you picking up a shift this weekend? Tomorrow will knock off number ten for me."

"I'm working a double tomorrow."

He lifted his hands. "You're a tough competitor."

"I want my life back. I can't wait to take Sam to the pool at our Disney resort. It has character fountains everywhere. I'll put on her life vest and just float with a cool drink."

"You're forgetting how much energy a five-year-old has." He leaned over her and pushed open her door. "I should have the lab results on Hobbs tomorrow. I'd like to rehearse my delivery with you."

No, he wanted to keep the conversation directed at any topic other than his family. Although he might disagree, she was going to save him. Because she was past the point of saving her heart.

She stepped to the curb but didn't close the door. "I can't figure out if you're being dishonest with me or yourself."

His smile melted. "I'm not dishonest about helping patients."

"Agreed. However, you're dishonest with your family. I think you're dishonest with yourself. You clearly love Sunberry. Why aren't you looking for a practice there? I'm sure they could use an oncologist."

He laughed. "Because it's too close to my big family."

She could swear there was a sadness in his tone, and she didn't think nostalgia produced it.

CHAPTER THIRTEEN

K yle drummed his fingers against the steering wheel until Dana disappeared inside the parking garage. He was not dishonest. Most of his colleagues found him painfully honest, which was the reason he needed her help to soften hard news. And he didn't lie to himself. Dana had no clue what it was like to grow up in a large family. If she did, she'd know how off the mark she'd hit.

His cheek spasmed. With a brusque movement, he scrubbed at his face. Sunberry was a great town. But the last thing he needed in his life was a constant reminder of his failure with Whit.

He threw his hands in the air. "So there, Dana Graham. I confess. I failed my brother."

The problem was living with failure. How could a man move past a failure when he had to meet his brother for coffee, sit with him at family dinners, or celebrate his new baby? Call him a coward, but he couldn't do that.

A car honked behind him, and he accelerated. Could he have a normal relationship with Whit once he'd made the payment? He shook off the question. Only time and a fat check written to Whit would determine if that were the truth or the real hidden lie.

On Monday morning, Kyle awakened energized and ready for the week despite working three overtime shifts. Dana had eased up on her family crusade, and he'd enjoyed three breaks with her. She'd shared funny stories about her early parenting mistakes with Sam and her daughter's mission to get a pet. The latest idea was a guinea pig. He'd looked up references online before getting some sleep. Sam was a cute kid, and he'd love to be the one to make her smile with a new pet—even if it landed him on Dana's fecal list.

Outside, he zipped his jacket and flipped on his bike lights. Soon, he'd need to tell her about his issue with Whit. She might cut him some slack if she understood how he felt about Whit. In the meantime, he needed a resolution because he wasn't going to jeopardize his relationship with Dana.

He lifted his leg over his bike. To be honest—he grinned —Dana would love the integrity reference after labeling him dishonest. The truth was, he couldn't mess up his relationship with her. She filled the vacuum left by avoiding his own family. Heck, she filled him, period. And he'd only kissed her once. Once they started dating like a real couple, she'd have him wrapped up and tied with a bow.

His legs pumped with his thoughts. He wanted to go on bike rides with her and Sam. Wanted to coach her daughter. Wanted to befriend George Graham and learn about the countless childhood stories that had formed Dana. He even wanted to take her home and let his big loving family fill the loss of her mother and sister.

"Just give me time, Cinderella. I'll figure out how to find your lost slipper."

Kyle groaned. Crap on a cracker, she had him talking out

his backside. He just needed more time to work things out with Whit.

The chime of his phone sounded while he was awaiting the elevator. Kyle moved inside the cubicle with a group of hospital staff and tugged his phone from his pocket. When he read Sarah Gates on his screen, his breath hung in his chest.

Sixty seconds later, he pumped his fist. Who needed an elevator? Nothing like good news to lift a guy. Man, he loved it when he could offer hope to a family.

By the time he finished his clinic appointments and rode the elevator to 6-West, his shirt felt too tight. Dana emerged from a patient room.

"I heard from Sarah." He couldn't suppress the wide grin, but good news needed a celebration. "Early or late lunch?"

Her smile faded. "That was fast. I guess they're back from their holiday."

"She sent me a text first thing this morning."

Dana checked her watch. "I'm on first lunch today."

"I'm making rounds. I'll meet you on the patio, same table if it's free." No way was her lack of enthusiasm going to spoil the mood. If Sarah's decision frustrated Dana, she could get over it. The decision belonged to Sarah. He pushed open his next patient's door. Maybe a piece of chocolate cake would return a smile to Dana's face.

Thirty minutes later, she entered the cafeteria while he approached the cafeteria cashier with his lunch. A frown continued to furrow Dana's smooth brow. Although he nodded at her, his stomach tightened into an unpleasant knot until he walked outside. The air, rich with the scent of earth and foliage, eased the tension in the back of his neck. Dana bent to dry her chair, hiking up her tunic top and showcasing a nicely rounded backside. Nothing like extracurricular images to refill the well. Uh-huh, Dana had a little meat on her, as Grandma Stella would say. But, man, did she wear it well.

If she'd noticed his prolonged stare, she ignored it, unloading her lunch from the frayed red lunch box.

"Let me guess?" He pulled out the webbed chair across from her. The distinctive aroma of salty peanuts filled the air. "Peanut butter?"

She picked up a flat bun filled with the tan paste. "With honey. My ambrosia."

He raised his glass of milk. "Here's to inexpensive meals."

"I like consistency." She pointed at his egg salad sandwich. "Take the egg salad. Does it have too much mayonnaise, mustard, pickle relish? You never know."

Man, he'd never get enough of her amazing blue eyes. Kyle opened his sandwich. He didn't even like the smell of pickles. "No relish."

When she laughed, he leaned against the back of his chair. Whatever had gotten her panties in a wad had dissipated—he hoped.

"You first," she said. "What did Sarah say?"

He straightened. "She asked me to coordinate a biopsy, which gives us time to run the labs and match treatments that might work for her."

"I didn't expect her to agree with treatment, but it's her decision," Dana said.

"So why the long face?"

She took too long to put down her sandwich. "Because Sam was disappointed I couldn't take her on a bike ride. I won't even be home to read her a bedtime story. How can I teach Sam to do the right thing when I keep letting her down, even when my intentions are pure?"

Her look twisted his heart. There was nothing worse than letting down a family member. He still suffered insomnia from his screwup with Whit.

"Hey." Unlike her chapped, over-washed palms, the flesh on the back of her arm glided soft and silky beneath his fingers. He'd bet the rest of her flesh would feel the same. "When I get down about an extra shift, I try to focus on the goal. I envision writing a final check to pay off my loans. I want to see nothing but zeroes."

A pathetic grin bowed her lips, which wouldn't do. Where was the brilliant smile that made him happy just to be around her?

He made a frame with his hands. "Picture this. The Dumbo ride is circling with you and Sam inside. Her laughter fills the air."

"You're right. She's excited about our trip. But you know kids? They live in the here and now. A month in the future to them is light-years away."

"In ten years, she won't remember missing a bike ride. She'll remember the first time she gets on the monorail or sees the parade with Mickey on the float."

She frowned. "Have you been to Disney World?"

Someday he'd learn to stop oversharing. "I have a little sister."

"So Dumbo was your favorite ride?"

"Space Mountain."

"But you've ridden Dumbo?"

She was enjoying this. He'd gladly down his dose of humiliation if it meant she'd smile. "I have a little sister."

"You also have two brothers and a mother."

Whit was always Hope's go-to brother, but he drew the line at two Dumbo rides, especially after riding It's a Small World with her. "Every one of us took a turn riding a dumb ride with Hope."

"So, did you do the teen attitude the entire ride?"

"Give me some credit. I wasn't a total jerk, and you should've seen the way her face lit up." Much like Dana's.

He'd always been a sucker for a girl's smile, especially after Mom had been sad for so long.

"You're right. My comment was unkind. You were amazing with the team and with Sam."

"Sam's a happy, well-adjusted little kid. You've done a good job."

Her cheeks turned rosy. Although he'd just been trying to step off the stupid pedestal she'd erected for him, he was glad he'd paid her the compliment. She worried too much. Sam was going to turn out just fine.

"Thanks."

When she nodded and looked away, a sudden empty feeling settled in his gut.

"Do you ever worry you believe something because you want to?" she said.

"I'm not sure what you mean," he lied. But he sure wasn't going to admit he'd ignored the risk to his brother because he liked the things Whit's money bought. Bile burned the back of his throat.

"I told you I was a helicopter mom after Mom and Robin's accident. I've been working to overcome it, but then I worry I'm overcompensating. What if I minimize something that needs attention?"

"So, you're afraid you'll miss something because you didn't dig deeper?" he said, finally getting the slant of her thoughts.

"My big sister was older and smarter. But I was determined to show Dad I was just as smart. If a question came up at the dinner table, I'd research the topic on warp speed to be the first to answer."

"I have two brothers," Kyle said. "Nate's the youngest. He'd do the same thing. I hated it."

"Sam pulled me and Dad through a dark time. Funny," she said, placing the riddled napkin into her lunch box with her remaining sandwich. "People try to protect kids from death.

But Sam accepted her favorite aunt had been taken from her. She was also the first to question if Mom liked lying in bed. She kept saying, 'Grandma doesn't like sleeping. She wants to get up.'"

Dana's voice hummed in the background, but he couldn't focus on her words. Instead, Sam's phrase repeated over and over in his head like one of Grandma Stella's scratched vinyl records. He shook his head, and the phrase ended, but he had no idea what Dana was talking about.

"How long was she in a coma?" he asked.

She paused and then huffed out a breath. "It took us seven months, five days, and seven hours to finalize the decision."

Kyle felt like one of those stupid bobbing heads, but he couldn't stop the motion. Just like he couldn't stop thinking about how painful it would be to watch someone you love continue in a vegetative state. Talk about losing hope. Day after day, waiting, praying there'd be a sign of the person you loved. Dana knew about losing hope. Maybe that's why she insisted on mending family rifts.

He started to ask her who made the decision to stop life support and hesitated. He already knew.

CHAPTER FOURTEEN

At 6:40 A.M. the following Friday, Dana stepped onto 6-West on a roll. She was Super Nurse, and she was invincible! Not. But her heart felt like it exceeded the circumference of her chest.

Things in the Graham household were stable. Although Sam continued her campaign for a pet—yesterday, it was a black poodle pup she'd found online—she also continued to grow into an amazing and generous spirit. The heaviness of grief had lifted from Dad too. He'd even started a garden. Then there was Kyle. Resisting the urge to perform a pirouette in the hall, she waved at the unit secretary, who was talking on the phone.

Dr. Kyle Murphy had proven to be a man of his word. Even his female patients had shifted their focus from Dr. Murphy, hot oncologist, to Dr. Murphy, compassionate oncologist with an amazing bedside manner. As suggested, he'd purchased business cards and pocket journals for his patients, who now contacted him with questions. Most of all, he'd slowed his approach. When he walked into a patient room, he pulled up a chair. He talked in an easy, down-to-earth manner. He listened, and the thoughtful, loving heart she'd witnessed shined through.

Dana hooked her purse in her locker. Although she'd played a part in his transformation, Kyle's changes came from within. He'd germinated like one of Dad's garden seeds. She'd merely provided a nourishing environment for his agile mind to grow. More impressively, he'd brought her to the sunshine with him.

She hesitated in front of the computer, the screen blinking with her patient assignment. She wanted more. But she couldn't risk her precious daughter, not until he'd resolved his family issues. According to her count of their competition, he was down to seven shifts. Although she didn't like the lines of fatigue bracketing his mouth, his push to the finish made her heart flutter. His desire to please her would do that to a gal.

At ten she joined most of the 6-West staff in the conference room for the case meeting. When Kyle joined five minutes later, her heart rate accelerated. She'd need to start working the cardiac step-down unit at this pace. Of course, since Kyle was the primary contributor, she had plenty of time to assess the case and her more sensual side.

When she stood to leave after the meeting, Kyle caught her eye and shifted his gaze to the left. That was her signal to hang back and let the team members exit. Too bad the delay subjected her to the flirt-with-Kyle banter that seemed to follow him like the plague. By the time he moved the last of his groupies out of the room, she was tapping her foot in irritation.

"Lunch?" he asked.

Only if you're on the menu. "Of course."

In the cafeteria, she followed Kyle, who carried his food to their usual patio table. She unloaded her usual fare from her lunch box.

When Kyle settled in the chair across from her, she hesitated. His cheek twitched again, which meant something was up. She removed her sandwich from the plastic bag, trying to remain calm.

He arranged his food. "One of the surgeons in ED told me about a park with a bike trail near here. He swore it's a great family place."

Dana's heart pounded in her ears, drowning out the redbird's chirp in the tree bordering the patio.

"I have a bike rack on my car," he continued despite her silence "What do you think about a picnic and a bike ride? Just you, me, and Sam."

Absolutely! Dana chewed slowly, hoping she didn't choke on her food since her throat felt like it was swollen closed. Yes, she wanted to be with him. Wanted to share a picnic and a bike ride with Sam. But could she be sure about his commitment?

If he kept up his current pace of four shifts a week, he'd talk to his family by the end of the month. What could it hurt to go on a picnic? Sam would be over the moon.

Dana chased her peanut butter with a gulp of water. It was her job to protect Sam, not give in to her hormones and fluttering heart.

A shadow changed Kyle's features. Disappointment, hurt?

"I've earned an honest answer," he said. "Just tell me I'm wasting my time, and we'll go back to a professional relationship, no harm, no foul. I'm a big boy. I can handle the truth."

She returned the uneaten half of her sandwich to the bag, careful to seal the zipper. "I believe you're a good man who would never deliberately hurt my daughter."

His tray scraped against the wire table when he pushed it aside. "I hear a 'but' coming."

Kyle's intuition had sharpened with her tutoring—probably too much. "I'm not worried about you hurting Sam." She stiffened. *Hello, Dana. Kyle's not the only one lying to himself.* "I'm more concerned about you hurting me."

He'd gone so still that she squinted to ensure he was breathing.

"The physical attraction has always been there for me," she admitted. "I knew the night we danced together. But physical attraction can wane with time. I'm older and wiser. I needed to learn your heart."

"If you know my heart, you should know I would never do anything to hurt you."

"That's what they all say." She smiled to soften her words.

"What a comfort to know I'm in the running with many."

"Why do you distance your family?"

Bull's-eye.

His scowl darkened his features. "My family has nothing to do with us. I care about you. You're smart, funny, and have a big heart. You've made me a better physician, a better man. Sure, it's fast and maybe a lot crazy. But we work together, we break together, we talk about our dreams and aspirations." He touched her hand, shaking his head. "That's not enough for me anymore. If you feel the same way, it's time to include Sam because I have this insane feeling we'll make an awesome trio."

Dana gripped the edge of the table. Say yes. She wanted to. But wanting something wasn't enough.

"I want that too," she whispered. "But relationships are built on trust. Show me I have yours by telling me about your family."

Furrows creased his forehead, pulling his heavy brows together. Had she crossed the line?

"The payment isn't for my education, at least not directly. Whit paid for my education. He doesn't need money, so it doesn't mean much to him. But I need to repay him. Once my debt's paid, I'll go home."

So he hadn't been totally honest with her. But was his repayment to Whit any different than her need to make her own house down payment? She didn't avoid Dad because he offered to help her finance her home. It was a simple "no, thanks."

"I lost half of my family in one fatal accident. One minute, we were planning to meet after a game, and the next, we were planning funerals."

"I agree. Family bonds are important. My family has done nothing wrong. The issue is with me and my debt to Whit. I haven't gone home because when I do, my issue makes everyone uncomfortable. That's not fair to my family or to Whit." He squeezed her fingers. "You've helped me see the way out of this. Now, you're as important to me as my family. That's why I'm working so many shifts. In a few weeks, I'll write Whit's check and take you and Sam to Sunberry for a weekend. You can meet the Murphy family—all of them."

Dana studied his handsome features. His tic didn't materialize, and his gaze remained steady, hopeful. That was Kyle, always striving to provide hope. Did she believe him, trust him, or was she fooling herself? His warm gaze and gentle touch clouded her thoughts. She'd drawn a line in the sand, and he'd been the first to reach out. In time, she'd learn more.

"Sam loves picnics and bike rides. With all the overtime, I've had to pass too many opportunities with her." She hesitated, hoping she was making the right decision. "Would it be okay if you join my family at the Spring Fling? Dad would be there to help buffer Sam's adoration of another male role model."

The tic twitched his cheek and she guessed she hadn't given the answer he wanted to hear. "I can compromise to make you happy."

She stood, kissed him on the cheek, and immediately regretted her rash behavior.

He grinned. "I'll be sure to compromise more often."

There was only one other occupied table, and no one was looking their way. Still... "I can't believe I did that."

"Surprised me too." He waggled his heavy brows. "But it was a nice surprise. Not that I haven't considered it. I just haven't acted on those thoughts."

"Too bad we don't work more evening shifts so you could walk me to my car."

"Just say the word."

She shook a finger at him. "I'm thinking you might be a bad influence on Sam. She's already an expert at getting her way."

"I'll take that as a compliment."

"You would. Back to the Spring Fling. What time is your dunking shift?"

He groaned. "Eleven to twelve. Paula scheduled me for the lunch period because she thinks staffers will spend money to get a shot at me."

"My BFF is not only a fantastic nurse manager. She's *dyn-o-mite* at targeting a fundraiser opportunity." It felt good to talk about something fun. "Sam will love throwing balls at the target."

"She's a baseball star. Of course, she'd get into that." Kyle pulled a fry from his abandoned plate. "I'm not worried about sitting behind the target for her. But have you seen some of the guys in radiology?"

"You're going to get wet." She giggled. "But don't discount Sam. She's been practicing her throwing arm with Dad. And she's developed a bottomless pit for a belly. My goodness, she eats as much as I do! Thank goodness I booked an all-inclusive plan for our Disney vacation."

"I'm sure my mother can relate. Me and my brothers could munch through the groceries. Before Mom remarried, I always felt guilty about eating too much."

That was sad. Since she'd already risked a kiss, she discreetly ran her pinkie along the back of his hand. His gaze found hers in moments.

He smiled. "Yes?"

"Maybe that's why our connection comes easily. We've both lost a parent too young," she murmured.

"I once took the people I loved for granted." His intense gaze burned into her soul. "Not anymore."

CHAPTER FIFTEEN

After finishing patient rounds Saturday morning, Kyle tapped the weather app on his phone. Super! The weatherman predicted a high temperature of sixty-eight degrees for his day in the pool. Add a light North Carolina breeze and his hour stint would chill his hide. Then again... A stupid grin cramped his cheeks. The afternoon with Dana would warm him. He pushed away from the unit counter and froze. *Back up, Murphy.* Seven overtime shifts still separated him from paying off Whit and starting a real life.

Instead of knocking off another shift, he was going to humiliate himself behind a target. He'd double down next week—unless Dana considered a real date with him. He slapped the top of the elevator and boarded. After all, a man couldn't work all the time.

An hour before his torture shift at the dunking pool, Kyle locked his bike at the neighborhood park Wilcox had secured for the Spring Fling. He followed the steady line of people beneath the colorful banner stretched over the entrance. The smell of popcorn and seasoned meat caused a rumble in his belly. His stomach obviously wasn't on board with delaying lunch until after his gig at the pool.

Too bad. He'd promised Dana a hot dog. A big smile pulled at his face. He rubbed his cheek. What was with his smiley face these days? He stopped, blinking at the assortment of carnival offerings. To his right, a large multicolored bounce house bobbled against its tethers. Squeals from kids competed with a different type of squeal. Kyle squinted at the backs of spectators filling temporary bleachers. Parked to the left of the bleachers stood a long white trailer with Pauly's Pronto Pigs decorating the side. Kyle snorted. He couldn't wait to take Sam to watch the pig races. No doubt, she'd lobby Dana for a piggy pet.

Strategically located near the tent featuring mouthwatering baked goods, pony rides, and the pie-throwing contest booth, loomed the dunking pool. Kyle grimaced when an athletic young man splattered whipped topping over a nurse from the ICU.

She licked her lips. "Banana cream. My favorite!"

The small crowd watching clapped their approval.

"He can't throw!" a man's voice through a grainy microphone sliced through the air.

Kyle pivoted toward the dunking pool. An ED nurse gave Paula a five for a bucket of balls. Joe Wood, a Wilcox internist, sat over the water.

"Get your towel ready," Kyle hollered. He'd worked with the nurse, and the guy was on a city baseball league. A moment later, the baseball hit the red star, and Joe splashed down.

"Hey, Doc!" Paula made change for the next participant. "Thanks for coming on time."

"You bet." Kyle shaded his eyes. "Any chance you heated the water?"

"Ask Dr. Wood. He's spent considerable time in it."

Kyle swallowed. He wanted the Spring Fling to raise a lot of money—just not by submerging him.

"Sales have picked up in the last thirty minutes." Paula held up a wad of bills. "We're going to hit our target."

Yippee! Maybe whoever bought the buckets of balls wouldn't hit theirs.

Twenty minutes later, Kyle shivered on the hardboard suspending him over the frigid tank water and spoke into the microphone. "Hey, Noodle Arm. You better lay down a twenty if you want to get my feet wet!"

The twenty-something guy escorting a nurse from the pediatric unit wound up for the pitch. Kyle held his breath, hoping his taunts and the guy's aim to impress his date would screw up his arm. Thwack! The ball smacked the canvas behind the target.

Close. Too close. But still a miss.

Kyle blew out a breath and checked his waterproof wrist-watch. Forty more minutes and he could escape the tank. The wet suit had been a good idea, but add a little breeze, and he was popsicle material.

While he taunted the players, he scanned the crowd for Dana. Two of the Triangle partners had passed and waved. He gave a salute. If they offered him a partnership, freezing his hide might be worth it. Maybe he should've signed up for the pie tent. He was starving.

He made sure there was always someone waiting to play a turn at his booth. Which wasn't hard. Since he knew many of the staff, a catcall could always stimulate a player.

His hour stretched into freaking forever. He rubbed his hand briskly through his hair to minimize the steady stream of cold water flowing down his neck. The crowd increased, but he hadn't seen a customer to shame into taking a shot at him.

He adjusted his prescription sunglasses and leaned left.

Dressed in a yellow sundress and dark glasses big enough to be goggles, Dana pointed in his direction. George Graham walked beside her, and dancing in front of her, Sam pointed at the pony ride.

Kyle chuckled. No doubt, Sam was suggesting a new pony pet. Dana should look for a house with land.

A ball grazed the target, causing Kyle's bench to tremor.

Yikes! A teenager, egged on by his buddy, started his windup. Kyle had played on a few high school teams to recognize the stance. Pitcher. With his luck, probably a good one. Kyle gulped a breath of air. Thwack! The board released and frigid water covered him. Bicycling his legs, he stood shivering.

"Looks cold," a male voice called.

He forced a smile and climbed back into position. "It is."

"Good thing they didn't set the tank under a tree," Dana responded.

"Grandpa, can I try?" Sam asked.

"Buy some balls, Dana," Kyle said, hoping for a break. With any luck, her daughter would burn up his remaining minutes.

Dana handed a five-dollar bill to Paula. When this was over, he'd have to kiss her for the save. He tightened his grip on the board. Maybe he'd kiss her just because she looked fine in her yellow dress.

Sam hopped from foot to foot while Dana set the bucket of balls in front of her.

"Okay, sport," Kyle called. "You can do this. Aim right at the round circle with the star in it."

When Dana bent to say something to her daughter, her hair seemed to blend into Sam's, so it was hard to tell where the girl stopped and the woman started.

Paula pulled up the rope, marking the throwing line, and directed Sam to walk closer.

"You just want to see me sputter one more time," Kyle protested. He didn't want to get dunked again, but he wanted Sam to be successful. Every kid needed a moment. With Mom and Grandpa looking on, what could be better?

"Hey," Paula said. "Sam's entitled to the youth line. Aren't you, sweetie?"

Sam grinned, revealing a hole where her right front tooth should be.

Thud. The ball caught the edge of the mat behind the target.

"Good arm," Kyle yelled. "A little more to the left."

"Throw it just like we practiced," Grandpa said from his position behind the rope.

Dana remained quiet, but she had the prettiest smile—the one that crinkled her eyes. He liked *it* best, but she seemed to hold it in reserve.

The second ball came in too low, but the third grazed the target.

"Super—"

Freezing water covered him, and he scrambled to find his footing on the bottom of the tank. Shivering, he stood. He hadn't seen Sam throw the last ball! Without his glasses, he couldn't see squat. Since his frames didn't float, he ran his big toe around the bottom of the tank. A familiar laugh cracked through the air just as his toe hit his frames. He should've known.

"Whit, you..." The word died on Kyle's tongue. Too many small ears listening to put his younger brother in his place.

"Pay attention, big brother." Whit cranked back his arm. "I bought a bucket of balls."

Thwack!

The board beneath him collapsed, but he caught the fall and kept his head above the surface. Shaking the water from his hair, he locked the seat and climbed into place.

Thwack!

Water sloshed over his face. How many balls were in a bucket? No doubt, Whit would hit the target every time.

"Are you reconsidering a comeback as a quarterback?" Kyle hollered.

Thwack!

At least Whit had the courtesy to wait for him to shake the water from his ears.

"Nope." Whit cranked his arm back for another throw. "But I've got to stay in shape for my little girl."

Thwack!

A cheering crowd surrounded the dunking pool. Did people like to watch a guy drown, or did they remember Whit's football days?

"Congratulations!" Kyle searched the faces for the orthopedic surgeon who had volunteered for the 12-1 shift. "Paula, is it—"

Thwack!

He wiped the water from his eyes and glanced at his wristwatch. 12:57 P.M.

He fiddled with the seat, counting off seconds in his head.

"You're getting slow, big brother," Whit called.

Kyle scrubbed the water from his eyes and straightened his glasses. Wow! Was that Talley? His sister-in-law had always been tall and lean. He raised a hand at her. Pregnancy suited her. Pretty and round, she looked amazing and very happy. Unlike the sad little girl she escorted to the youth line with Sam.

Whit sat the bucket of balls between Sam and the little girl. "Bringing in the first string," Whit hollered. "They're going to throw the rest of the balls I bought."

"Sorry, Dr. Murphy," Paula whispered from the other side of the tank. "I hope you don't mind. I agreed you'd stay in the tank until the man with the pregnant lady threw the entire bucket. He donated five hundred dollars."

"I'm sure he did," Kyle muttered through the frozen smile he displayed to the crowd. "But I'll get more out of him later. Promise."

"Sam's his designated pitcher," Dana called, her face cheerful.

A surprising warmth stopped Kyle's shivers, and he tightened his lips to suppress the smile. His brother looked ... good. Unlike the man who had starred on the sports magazine covers, Whit, kneeling to help the two kids, fit the father role. It matched his personality.

His seat quivered from Sam's weak but accurate pitch. Kyle's smile slipped free. If his brother could fit the role, why couldn't he?

"Give it your best windup," Kyle said, but he couldn't hide the smile. Man, he'd missed family life.

CHAPTER SIXTEEN

B eside the tank, Dana suppressed a laugh. She was right
about needing a day off, and Kyle was right about
including Sam and Dad. Meeting Whit and Talley was an
added delightful surprise.

Although she'd noticed the tall man with his pregnant
partner, she hadn't identified them as Whit and Talley until
he'd started teasing Kyle. Bulkier than his brother, Whit
shared the same confident posture. Well, duh. The guy had
hit the target with every ball, which was pretty funny.

Even if she hadn't known about Kyle's brother, the under-
tone of sibling rivalry between them gave them away. Both
men sported a snarky grin that lifted her heart. There was
nothing like fun between siblings. Kyle was lucky to have
them. She didn't know the conflict between the brothers, but
it couldn't be permanent, not with the behavior she was
witnessing.

Talley, dressed in a T-shirt emblazoned with "Bunny on
board" and black tights, egged on the brothers. A twinge of
jealousy touched Dana's shoulders. She'd never looked that
good during her pregnancy. But it was more than physical

beauty. Talley glowed with happiness and love, a stunning combination.

Since Talley was carrying her first child, the little girl at her side must be a cousin. The tiny hairs on Dana's forearms lifted. Something was wrong. Although precious, the little one seemed ...sad. No, sad was too light. A memory of a patient washed over her. Like her patient, the child appeared devastated.

"Do you want to try?" Sam held out a ball to the little girl. "It's kind of hard. But I hit the target once."

Tears stung Dana's eyes. Her sweet Sam instinctively empathized with the girl. Her breath stalled in her chest at the kindness in her daughter's voice.

"Good job, Sam," she murmured. Although her voice was too low for Sam to hear, she needed to say the words to keep from hugging her daughter to her chest.

The sad little girl blinked at Sam, then stared down at her outstretched hand.

"Give it a try." Sam's narrow shoulders lifted and fell. "I'm just learning to throw too. Grandpa has been helping me."

"OMG," Talley whispered. "Is she yours?"

Dana nodded, her heart too full to speak.

"I'm Talley Murphy. And the little sweetheart is Noel."

Noel? Dana bit her lip. Little angels should never experience heartbreak. Sam, oblivious to the adult spectators, proceeded to give Noel precise directions on holding the ball.

"Her dad was killed last week during an accident on base," Talley whispered. "My husband Whit and I brought her with us to give her family time to make funeral arrangements and to give her a fun day away from the sadness. She's spoken very little for two days."

Dana swallowed. She'd been going blissfully through her day with her healthy family, and Noel had been living with the sudden loss of her dad. Poor child. Life could be harsh.

Another reminder to live in the moment, appreciate the gifts surrounding her. Love Sam. Love Dad. Enjoy a beautiful day of sunshine. She blinked back the threat of tears. Do everything possible to help others who are not having such a good day.

In front of her, Sam performed her best pitcher move. "Then you rear back like this and throw it as hard as you can."

The ball hit the edge of the target with a little thump, the seat vibrated, and Kyle slid into the water.

"Did you see that? Did you see that?" Sam raised her arms in the air. "I did it."

Dad cheered, along with the small crowd. Talley grinned and whispered in Whit's ear. When he turned to look at his wife, Dana swallowed. This was a man who wore his love for his wife on his face. What would it feel like to know that kind of love?

Sam grabbed another ball from the bucket. At first, Dana thought she was going to try again. Instead, she handed it to Noel.

"You can do it," Sam said.

"She's going to try," Talley whispered.

Noel touched the ball and then opened her hand and pointed to something in her palm. Dana stood on her toes but couldn't make out what held Noel's attention.

"What's that?" Sam asked.

"Daddy's rock," Noel said.

"Do you want me to hold it so you can throw the ball?"

Talley leaned closer to Dana. "Whit organized a charity that mentors children who lose a parent."

Whit gave her a smile.

In front of the dunking pool, Noel paused, looking from the ball to the rock in her palm. "Don't drop it," she said after a moment. "It's special."

"I won't," Sam promised.

Noel mimicked Sam's motion, but the ball fell a few feet in front of the target.

Dana's throat thickened. Sam, who had never known her father, was helping Noel through the loss of hers. Life never ceased to amaze her, just as the wonderful little soul given to her.

While the kids continued to go through the bucket of balls, Talley provided more details about her husband's mission to help the children of fallen veterans.

"That's an amazing story," Dana said. Kyle mentioned Whit was generous, but this was more than giving money. Like Kyle, Whit gave with his heart.

"Whit's going to make an awesome dad." Talley pressed her hand to his chest, a tender expression of love on her face. "And so will his brothers. Their mother Ava instilled so much love into the Murphy men."

Beside her, Noel missed again, and Sam provided more instructions.

Talley cradled her small baby bump. "In case you missed it, Whit and the guy on the hot seat are brothers. I couldn't imagine celebrating this birth without Kyle. He's an oncologist here. Since he's so busy, we came to make a personal plea. Plus, Kyle told us he was volunteering today, and we had a little one who needed a distraction."

Aha, now the picture was coming into focus. She offered her hand. "Dana Graham. Kyle and I work on the oncology unit together. And of course that's my amazing daughter Samantha. However, she only answers to Sam."

"Sam fits her," Whit said. "You've raised her right. Noel needed a friend to show her kindness."

"Thanks. I try." Dana smoothed the hair from her face. "I take it Kyle didn't know you were coming?"

"Nope, not until Whit smacked the target." Talley

lowered her voice. "My husband was an NFL wide receiver. I had no idea he could hit a target with a baseball."

"I think it's awesome."

Talley's eyes widened. "How long did you say you've known my brother-in-law?"

Dana moistened her lips. No way was she going to lie to Kyle's sister-in-law, and she'd already decided she liked her, so she gave Talley an abbreviated version of her relationship with Kyle.

"So," Talley shaded her face and studied Kyle. "You're helping Kyle with his communication skills? That must be an interesting task."

Several responses tickled the tip of Dana's tongue. "Very."

"Based on the timing, I'm guessing I have you to thank for the recent responses I've received from Kyle."

Dana wasn't sure of the answer, so she remained silent. The girl's missed the target, and Whit slipped under the rope to talk to them. Dana guessed it was something fun because even Noel grinned.

"Ready? One, two, three, go!" Whit shouted.

Sam and Noel charged the tank and pushed the target. Kyle splashed into the water.

"And they score!" Whit shouted, kneeling to high-five Sam and Noel. "You two are awesome. I want you on my team at the baby party. Deal?"

"I hope you and Sam will consider coming," Talley said. "Noel needs friends, and this is the first time since the accident that she's come out of her shell. Sunberry is an easy drive east and it's a lovely town. Since you're working communication skills magic with my hardheaded brother-in-law, I'd be forever grateful if you could deliver him to the shower." She smiled sweetly. "I'm not opposed to the use of force."

"Ha!" A bubble of laughter escaped Dana. Although she slapped her hand over her mouth, Kyle squinted in her direction. This was crazy. She didn't know Talley or Whit, and who crashed a baby shower? Well, Talley had invited her. She finger-waved to Kyle. It would be interesting to meet his family. OMG, she'd lost her mind.

"That's um, very generous of you," Dana said. "But—" What? She was planning to work an extra shift, the same as Kyle. The idea tingled through her and quirked her lips. "Let me get back with you."

"Looks like Aunt Catherine has also found a friend." Whit canted his head to the left.

Dana followed his movement. "Dad?" This day was seriously weird.

"Is he the man talking to the lady in the blue tunic and the white capris?" Whit asked.

Dana blinked. He was also the man with a huge grin on his face. He'd been slowly improving...until this leap! Had Whit asked a question? Dana managed to tip her chin. Wow. Crazy day.

Talley grinned. "Is your dad, by any chance, single?"

"Yes," Dana said. But her voice sounded like she'd fallen in the pool with Kyle, who was talking with his replacement.

"Another Murphy strikes." Talley beamed. "Aunt Catherine is a widow and never met a stranger. This must be a serendipity event."

Whit kissed Talley's cheek and then shook his head. "Don't mind my wife. Pregnancy has messed with her brain cells. Her doc assured me she'd be back to normal after delivery."

"You're all coming," Talley said. "Please. Begging looks bad on a pregnant woman, but if necessary, I'll do it. Besides, I've got Whit to help me up from my knees."

Dana removed her sunglasses and cleaned them on her dress hem, but her vision still seemed...fuzzy. A Murphy whirlwind had engulfed her. It started the evening she'd danced with Kyle and hadn't stopped.

Warm hands wrapped around her fingers. Dana blinked at Talley's big smile. Although they'd just met, Kyle's sister-in-law put her at ease. Made her feel as if they were best friends, like a sister. Crazy, but Whit also had a comforting effect on her. Not Kyle. Getting through his tough exterior had required work.

"Have you eaten yet? Noel could use a friend, and we"— Talley waved Whit over. "Could use a buffer while we plead our case to Kyle. It wouldn't surprise me if he makes an excuse to avoid us."

Dana swallowed. Kyle needed to talk with his brother, but Talley and Whit had come to see him, not her. And Dad? He hadn't socialized since Mom died.

"Hey." Kyle's familiar voice came from behind her. He adjusted a striped beach towel around his dripping body. "I see you've met Talley."

Talley hugged Kyle and didn't release him until he placed his arms around her in return.

Dana hid a smile. She knew she liked Talley.

"You're going to drown my niece before she arrives." Kyle gently backed away from Talley, his cheeks red, but a smile breaking his stern features.

"The Murphy family needed more women to offset the testosterone," Talley said.

Kyle cuffed Whit's shoulder. "Way to go, bro. Congratulations! That's awesome."

"Excellent." Talley held up two fingers. "That means we can count on you to come to the baby shower. First, you're joining us for lunch."

When Kyle's grin faded, Dana resisted the urge to pinch him. Whatever caused his prickly behavior was clearly one-sided. He was going to lunch, and if she had a say, to the shower, even if she had to drag him there, kicking and screaming.

Kyle shook his head. "Sorry, but this is the hospital's largest fundraiser. I have to stay and support it."

"Perfect," Talley said, never missing a beat. "Sam and Noel have already made a connection, and so have Aunt Catherine and Dana's dad. How about we meet"—Talley checked her phone— "at the bounce house in fifteen minutes?" She smiled at Noel and Sam. "Do you like the bounce house?"

Sam cheered, and even quiet Noel giggled.

Talley beamed. "I guess it's settled. Change your clothes and meet us there."

Kyle frowned. "Talley—"

"Sweetheart." Aunt Catherine sidestepped Talley and wrapped her arms around Kyle. "You're working too hard. You've lost weight."

Dana pressed her fingers to her lips to hide her grin. Although not as tall as Talley, Catherine had a similar presence. The Murphy women, regardless of blood, created a force of nature. Her kind of women. Kyle might as well give up because he was out of his element and losing ground fast.

"Aunt Catherine." Kyle wrapped his arms around the woman, a big happy grin changing his features. "You look amazing."

Dana blinked. A happy version of Kyle? She'd seen it at the ball game coaching the kids and now with his family. This was the cheerful Kyle, the unguarded Kyle. The man who's untethered by life-and-death decisions. This man, with the dimple winking at her, drew her like a butterfly to a flower. A flutter moved through her belly.

"And this—" Catherine extended her arm. "Is my new friend George Graham. Now, we know one another. When's lunch?"

Another little jolt kicked up Dana's heartbeat. Dad's smile

matched Kyle's. Holy smokes, Murphy happiness was contagious.

"It's settled," Whit said.

Kyle stiffened beside her, but Whit didn't seem to notice. Dana lifted her chin. Kyle was not going to spoil the day with whatever ancient history he'd created with his brother. Families were precious, even with their warts exposed. He might object, but no way could she walk away without helping him see the importance of family. He might even thank her someday.

Fifteen minutes later, she felt certain he wouldn't thank her for agreeing to attend Talley's shower with Sam and Dad. All she had to do now was persuade Kyle to join them. Based on his scowl, that might be a challenge.

"I knew I was going to like Talley." Dana wove her arm through Kyle's.

She might as well have dunked him in the pool again. His eyes widened, and there was a slight delay before he snapped his gaping mouth closed.

Dana hid a smile. Then again, this challenge could be fun. "She's going to make an awesome mother. Your brother is a lucky man."

Sam tugged on the side of her dress. "Mom, can I go to the aquarium?"

"Excuse me," she warned.

"Excuse me." Sam moistened her lips and smiled sweetly. "Can I? Whit said they have sharks there."

Kyle's scowl returned.

Talley guided Dana away while Whit diverted Sam and Noel. "Please let Sam come with us. I promise we'll take great care of her. We rented a condo near the aquarium for the night. We're driving there this evening, so we'll have all morning to visit the exhibits. We'll have her back tomorrow late afternoon, at the latest."

"Talley," Kyle started.

However, his sister-in-law launched into the reason for Noel's presence. Kyle's gaze roved from Sam, standing hand in hand with Noel, to watching Whit shoot baskets to win a stuffed toy.

"Every child needs a friend, especially when they're sad," Dana murmured.

Unlike her, Sam didn't have brothers or sisters or even cousins. Her heart squeezed. But maybe someday....

"We can meet you halfway if you can wait until after I get off." Dana glanced at Kyle, but he was staring at the kids.

"I didn't know about Whit's work with children," he said.

Dana squeezed his forearm. He'd missed too much about his brother. Maybe she'd share her observations—later.

She swallowed. Since Sam was going to the aquarium, she had an entire night to persuade Kyle to resolve his conflict with Whit. An entire night alone with him.

CHAPTER SEVENTEEN

K yle shoved his fists in his pockets. Today was a perfect example of why he avoided visiting Sunberry. Aunt Catherine and George laughed and photographed the kids like old lovers. He needed sunglasses to protect his eyes from the love-light radiating from Whit and Talley. Crashing the feel-good reunion was his sorry mug, Jerks"R"Us. Not that he wanted to be the storm cloud ruining the picnic. It seemed to come on as a side effect every time he was around family.

His fake smile wasn't fooling anyone, especially Dana. Sure, she continued her usual cheerful demeanor, but disappointment dulled the sparkle in her eye. George Graham had discreetly shot him speculative looks all afternoon. Dana's dad would probably advise her to drop him like a cold turd tonight.

Worse, he couldn't explain the weird sensations assaulting him. The unreasonable fear his brother was a walking time bomb made Kyle feel a little crazy. Whit's every movement sent an electric bolt to his heart.

Whit stumbled over a cable, and an X-ray of a bone riddled with early arthritis flashed in Kyle's mind. Every time

Whit hesitated or mispronounced a word, an image of a brain desiccated by Chronic Traumatic Encephalopathy haunted him. What about his new niece? Would her father be healthy enough to play with her, protect her, father her?

Kyle understood the hazards of professional football better than anyone. Yet he'd said nothing. Just let his kind, generous brother take all the risks while he'd taken his money. Blood money. What kind of man did that to the brother he was supposed to mentor, protect? He felt like last year's trash. He'd earned that feeling, which is why he had to make it better for his family. Doing that would be hard. Telling Dana would be devastating.

An hour after Whit and Talley departed, and George had stunned everyone by inviting Aunt Catherine to stay for a night of dancing, Kyle's self-disgust eased. Since Whit had sunk enough baskets to win a stuffed rabbit for Noel, Kyle approached a dart-game vendor.

"Is Sam still on the pet kick?" He rolled his shoulders.

"Don't remind me." Dana adjusted her floppy hat. "This week, it's a hedgehog. If the preschool invited the student population to share their pets one day, they'd probably win a prize for the largest variety of animals. I mean, really. Who owns a hedgehog, other than folks on the Internet?"

Kyle handed the vendor a five-dollar bill for six darts. "Do you think she'd settle for a stuffed Golden Retriever?"

When she tilted her head to check out the huge toy dog dangling above her, the long column of her neck tempted him. What was with him today? He'd always been a man of science. Give him black-and-white facts. Today, however, he'd transitioned into a dreamer. First, scary images of Whit, and now, sensual images of Dana. He thumped his palm against the side of his head. It didn't do squat to dislodge the daydream.

Dana rewarded him with a genuine smile. It had been hours since she'd done that. "Can't hurt to try."

"Don't hold your breath." He picked up a dart, testing the weight. "I was pretty good in college—like a gazillion years ago. If I've lost my touch, we can stop at the mall tomorrow and buy Sam a stuffed toy before we meet Whit."

Way to go, Murphy. Screw up with a little girl and buy your way out, just like your brother.

He cocked his arm. The first throw missed the bull's-eye but stuck in the 25. The following five hit the bull's-eye.

"Did we win?" Dana's excited tone lifted his funk.

The vendor pointed to the second level. "Choose anything hanging on tier two."

Kyle's smile evaporated. He couldn't even win a decent toy for Sam. "Sorry, I didn't come through for her."

"We'll take the little duck," Dana said. "She'll love it."

Too bad he couldn't give her daughter what she really wanted, a living, breathing animal to show her love. It seemed like he was coming up short for everyone he cared about.

By the time they circled the carnival, the sun had settled beneath the horizon. Twinkle lights outlined the Wilcox tent, and speakers emitted the first strains of a rock song. On the breeze, the tempting aromas of cotton candy, popcorn, and fried pastries beckoned.

Kyle took Dana's hand, marveling at the fit of her warm fingers. "Do you want another corn dog?"

"Absolutely not! One yummy footlong with extra mustard is my limit." She winked. "But I wore dancing shoes."

Kyle side-eyed the strappy yellow sandals matching her dress. "Of course you did since I'm such an awesome dancer."

Instead of laughing at his lame attempt at humor, she followed him to the temporary dance floor and raised her arms. His heart thumped so fast he questioned his physical stamina. Thank goodness his body held up because he'd never wanted to hold anyone like he wanted, no needed, to hold Dana. Her cinnamon scent filled his head, and he sent a silent thank-you to Whit.

The irony emerged in a light grunt. A thank-you was the last thing on his list when Whit tried to drown his butt in the dunking pool. However, he owed his brother big-time for a night alone with Dana. No, he owed his brother, period.

Tall for a woman, Dana fit perfectly beneath his chin. His flesh twitched. Don't turn it off. Keep playing the same song and let him slowly sway her body to the music's rhythm. When the ballad progressed to the chorus, he spun her to the right, using the movement to snug her closer. Her fragrance engulfed him. A contented sigh leaked through his lips. The next time he ate cinnamon bread, he'd probably visualize rumpled bedsheets.

On the dance floor to his right, he watched Paula's date kiss her temple. Kyle's chest seized, and he just missed Dana's foot. That's all he needed. Her slender toes, with their pink nails, wouldn't stand a chance beneath his boat-sized deck shoes. When he pivoted, her dress brushed against his khakis. An image of sturdy-muscled calves burned into his mind, reducing the carnage of a broken foot.

He was a jerk. But not about Dana. Not anymore. At the award ceremony, he'd thought she was special and then run like a coward at the first mention of a child. Sweet little Samantha Graham made Dana special, had forged her into a caring mother. He'd been stupid and self-serving, just like his excuse to get out of attending Whit and Talley's shower.

Kyle spun her to the left, holding her close. When she missed a step, he tightened his grip to steady her—just like he wanted to do for the rest of his life. Full disclosure? She steadied him, sharpened his focus, opened his heart. Regressing to the self-centered jerk she'd first met was no longer an option.

"I've got you, beautiful." The first time he'd spoken those words to her, they'd sounded cheesy. Now, they sounded perfect. At least they weren't a canned line from a guy looking to make a pass. Although he wouldn't protest if she agreed to spend the night with him.

"At first, I thought you were just another sweet-talking guy," she said on a sigh. "But I've learned you have a very giving heart. Talley said your mother raised you with a lot of love."

He misstepped. If she knew what he'd done to Whit, she'd call him something very different. Swallowing, he shoved the thought to the back of his mind. Tonight, they were together. Tonight, she liked him, respected him. No way would he jeopardize it. Everything might blow up in his face down the road, but not tonight.

"And I was doing so well." He lifted his shoulder. "I'm out of practice."

"Too many extra shifts." Her voice barely carried above the music, but the movement of her mouth held his attention.

When the tip of her tongue moistened her lips, his lungs seemed to freeze. Was something worrying her? He should ask. Later. They could talk on the drive to meet Whit or at next shift's lunch. But not tonight. He didn't want to do anything to break the spell.

The music faded. *Get with it, DJ. I'm not letting her go.*

"My Cinderella," he whispered.

The twinkle lights danced in her eyes. "This is nice," she murmured.

He kissed her hair, glad she'd removed the hat. "I'm enjoying the moment."

In the lull between songs, his heart thundered in his ears. He'd be a fool to say or do anything to lose this incredible woman.

The rapid-fire beat of the next song blasted through the speakers. She leaned back in his arms, her gaze lancing him, her Cheshire grin pulling him from the haze.

"We're out of step." Her eyebrow raised.

He guided her away from the dance floor, waved at Aunt Catherine and George, and continued from the tent.

"Your dad looks like he's enjoying himself," Kyle said.

"That is such a relief." Dana's words rushed out, which was unlike her.

"Is that okay?" Although he didn't want to talk about her dad or his family, he'd vowed to leave Jerk Kyle behind.

"This is going to sound selfish."

Yeah, he had the target on that one. "But—"

Her chuckle created a lifting sensation in his belly like he was taking off in a jet—a very fast jet. Still, no complaining, regardless of the topic. No work, no daughter, no diversions. Just Dana and the night. If she wanted to talk about rampant fungi, he'd listen. Well, maybe he'd fantasize about her during the discussion. But he'd pretend to listen.

"I felt guilty about wanting my own place," Dana said. "Dad sold his home in Blowing Rock and moved here to help me with Sam."

"He's proud of your success. It's a wonder he doesn't pound his chest every time you walk in the room." He sure wanted to.

Laughter drifted in the mild evening air. Too bad he didn't have a blanket so they could lie beneath the stars. He snorted.

Dana tugged his hand. "What's that about?"

"A random dumb thought." He was not going to share. "You were talking about feeling guilty."

"It's just...Dad's okay, and he's not that old. I mean, he's my dad."

Kyle stopped at his car and opened the door for her. "I think Aunt Catherine has a different perspective."

Dana slid into the passenger seat, the hike of her dress revealing a creamy thigh. "You have a lovely family."

There was nothing wrong with his family. Soon enough, she'd learn it was him. He squeezed his eyes closed. *Turn it off, Murphy. Live in the moment.*

When he slipped behind the wheel, her smoky expression singed his throat—and it wasn't heartburn.

"Where are we going?"

Any place you want. He leaned across the slushbox and kissed her. "I figured the staff would talk if we made out at the dance."

Her grip on his shirt prohibited pulling away. Like he wanted to. He cradled her chin in his palms. "How'd I get so lucky to be here with you?"

"I'd say we owe your brother and sister-in-law."

"Don't spoil the moment." He kissed her slow without opening the seam of her lips. It nearly killed him.

When he broke the kiss, she nipped his lip, sending a jolt of desire through him.

Oblivious to what her kiss had fueled down south, she settled back in her seat and fastened the seat belt. "Let's finish this conversation at my place. Oh, we're not working tomorrow. I pulled my availability for extra shifts."

He liked the way she thought. The Subaru purred to life at the switch of the key. "I could work a shift and surge ahead. You'd have a hard time catching up."

"I don't want to compete with you."

Although the shadows hid her feelings, the softness of her voice alerted him of a change. He moistened his lips. "What do you want?"

More importantly, what did he want? Was he ready to reveal it to her, to himself?

"You."

He gripped the steering wheel. "Hold that thought. I can't have this conversation and drive."

At the intersection adjacent to the hospital, he pressed the brake. "Are we going to discuss the agreement terms before we reach your place?"

"Are you worried I'll mess with your decision-making?"

"Heck, yes!"

Dana tilted her head to the side and eyeballed him like Mom used to do when he or his sibs told fibs.

A comeback line circled his mind, but he didn't speak. This wasn't a time to swap punch lines. They'd reached a crossroads. Sure, he wanted to kiss her, let her voice vibrate through him, touch her hair. But his body had jumped ahead somewhere between a dance and a kiss. They weren't two teenagers who let hormones dictate decisions, especially decisions that impacted Sam.

The little imp had been so cute showing Noel how to throw the ball. He'd never do anything to jeopardize her happiness. And her mother? His breath rushed across his lips. He'd do anything for her. Wanted to do everything for her.

Don't go there, at least not yet. But how lucky could a guy get? Even a douchebag, who had ridden on his little brother's checkbook, caught an occasional break. Still, a man didn't start a treatment without knowing the diagnosis. He focused on driving the car. Except he kept a secret watch on her. Once he caught a twitch of her left hand beneath a streetlight, but she didn't make a move. Which was a blasted shame.

"I want to know more about you." *Not more, Murphy, everything.* What was her favorite food? What made her happy? What was she thinking when she got that distant look in her eye?

Ten minutes later, he stopped in front of her cottage. The

Subaru's engine idled beneath the giant oak. Her home beck-oned. He swallowed. Waited. Dana had the most at risk. He'd already lost himself to her. Until tonight, he hadn't known it.

"You said you were ready to take the next steps." Dana unbuckled her seat belt and turned to face him. "What does that mean?"

Was she asking about the L word? How could he answer when he didn't know? He only knew he wanted to be with her, make her happy.

"I've spent my life studying science, anatomy, physiology, but this...?" He shook his head. "All I can tell you is you're the earworm repeating in my head. I can't remove you." His throat tightened. "I don't want to."

In the ambient light from her porch, her eyes seemed like dark saucers in her face. He felt frozen, suspended in time.

"Dana?" His hoarse whisper sounded distant.

When her fingers brushed his jaw, the vise crushing his chest eased.

"Thank you for your honesty," she said. "I like knowing I can count on that trait."

He placed his hand over hers. "That's the thing. I like everything about you." He touched her lips with his. "Even the maddening way you stand your ground."

"And push you to change your perspective?"

"That's your worst and best trait."

"Be gentle with us," she said. "Sam looks at you with adoration. I've already earned a few scars on my heart. But I'm not looking for more."

"I'd forfeit a limb before I hurt either of you."

Her smile held a hint of sadness. "I believe you mean those words. But we can't predict the future."

"No, we can't." He folded her smaller hands in his. "But I think we're...," He kissed her knuckles. "*This* is worth the risk."

"No sleepovers with Sam."

"Never," he said.

"Honesty first, even when it's harsh and brutal."

"I couldn't be harsh with you. But I'll be honest. I want you in my life. I'm not sure what that looks like, what works for you."

She slid her hands around his neck, sending an array of impulses through his body. "Kiss me."

"Thought you would never ask."

His mother had taught him tenderness, but tender didn't describe Dana tonight. Her lips searched, sucked while her tongue dueled with his. The soft sounds coming from the back of her throat urged him to accelerate, intensify. The hands that attended the sick tempted and teased.

He released her mouth and pressed his forehead to hers while the rasp of their breathing filled the interior. The urge to feel her flesh against his surged through him. He didn't move. After a moment, she straightened in her seat.

"I think it's time to go inside," she said.

Just follow her lead and keep your mouth shut. "Are you sure?" He cringed, but he promised honesty, and she had to want this as much as he did.

She opened the passenger door and then winked at him over her shoulder. Winked! Who knew such a simple gesture would arrow straight to his groin? He clenched his fists to keep from racing to the door. She made him want to chuck his plans out the window and follow her down the yellow brick road to his fantasies.

"Dr. Murphy." Did her hand tremble when she unlocked the door? She led the way inside. "You have a lustful gleam in your eye."

Ya' think? "It's all your fault."

He moved in behind her, unable to resist the curve of her back and the slope of her shoulder. He slid his arms around her waist, loving when she quivered beneath him. Her scent tingled the back of his tongue. Although desire fired his veins, another softer vibe slowed his movements. He nestled closer to her. Dana grounded him, relieved the constant anxiety surging through him.

He rubbed his cheek against her shoulder. "Don't move."

"Kyle?"

He chuckled. "Your weird boyfriend is having a moment. Men have them too, you know."

She turned to face him, her eyes sparkling with humor. "Do tell."

"I was kind of bummed about my gig in the dunking pool. Then you showed up in a floppy hat and big sunglasses—"

"You liked them?"

Not near as much as he liked her smile. "I did." He kissed the tip of her nose to slow the pace. "Great look."

"I was disappointed you didn't wear a Speedo."

She could always make him laugh. "I wasn't. They filled the tank with a fire hose. The water was frigid."

She slid her hands up his chest. "Do you want me to adjust the thermostat?"

"Ahh, no. I'm having a hard enough time adjusting to being alone with you. I never imagined my night would end like this. Can we get back to the kissing?"

Before he could move, she leaned in, kissed him. Her lips barely brushed his, featherlight. He dropped his forehead against hers, his mind a collage of input: the scent of cinnamon, the satin of her skin, and the gallop of his heart.

Her gaze flickered like the twinkle lights from the dance.

"One test is not enough evidence." He grazed her lips, lingering for almost too long.

She glanced to the right and lifted a brow. "Thanks to your brother we have the night to ourselves."

"Your dad?"

"He'll see your car."

"I get you're a consenting adult, but it will feel weird the next time I see him."

Dana laughed. The rich sound echoed in her tight living quarters. He meant to give her another soft kiss, but she sighed into his mouth and touched his tongue with hers. His head felt like it might blow off, and his hands roved from her jaw to the fine column of her neck, the silkiness of her hair, the rounded muscle of her shoulders. It nearly killed him, but he released her lips and took her hands.

"We've got two choices: I can kiss you goodnight and get in my car. Or..."

Her right brow lifted. "Or?"

"We can continue this trial in your bed." Kyle shook his head. "Your body language is killing me."

She pulled his face closer. "Then you have all of the clinical evidence you need."

"I want you to be sure you understand the outcome."

She ran her tongue along his lip line. "You have yet to disappoint me."

A tiny voice in the back of his mind urged him to hurry before he did.

KYLE SPOONED Dana closer to the curve of his body, breathing in the smells of her perfume, sex, and an unidentifiable sweetness. Dana was amazing. The sex was unbelievable, but he couldn't shake the ticking-bomb feeling. Worse, he didn't know where to find the fuse.

He should thank his stars for the opportunity to be with someone like Dana. He shook off the funk. "Now, I get why you need a home of your own."

She repositioned to face him. "Twin beds are cozy. But I could live without the bubblegum odor."

"Is that what's causing the smell?"

"Yes." She kissed him on the cheek and sat on the side of the bed. "I don't let Samantha chew gum, so she's gone to a lot of trouble to hide it."

Dana turned on the bedside lamp, and ten tiny roses with light centers illuminated the small bedroom.

Kyle retrieved his boxer briefs. "Maybe it's payback for the no-pet policy."

Dana disappeared into the bathroom and returned wearing a worn blue T-shirt. "Can I get you something to drink? A snack?"

"Water."

He followed her into the open living quarters. "For a single guy, a one-bedroom cottage is perfect. With its open eating, living, and kitchen, the space is efficient. But for two, I see how it's a tight fit."

"I'm really looking forward to a regular bed." She looked over her shoulder and winked. "However, the twin mattress worked nicely for us."

"No complaints from me." Except he didn't get to spend the night with her.

She retrieved two bottles of water from the refrigerator and sat opposite him on the scarred coffee table, her knees touching his. "I've got a confession to make, and I'm not quite sure how to break it to you."

The hairs along his neck lifted. He should've dressed while he had the chance.

She huffed out a little breath, causing her breasts to jiggle beneath her shirt. "I want to attend Talley's shower with Dad, Sam,...and you."

Really? She wanted to talk about that now? She'd probably been thinking about the shower while—No. Based on the moans and sounds she'd made, that wasn't possible. At least he hoped not. If so, it didn't say a lot for his abilities in bed. He shifted on the lumpy futon.

She was watching him, waiting for a response. What could he say? It wasn't like he was going to act like a jerk and refuse to go.

"Before you lose your mind." She raised her palm. "Hear me out."

Since he couldn't trust some smart-aleck response wouldn't pop out of his mouth, he nodded.

"You know I think you should attend, but this isn't a ploy to corner you. It's Noel." Her shoulders heaved. "She lost her dad, Kyle. If Sam can ease her pain, even for an afternoon, we have to go."

Leave it to Dana to go straight for the jugular. He massaged his forehead. Hope had been too little to feel the impact of his dad's death, but he and his brothers had. That's probably why Whit had gotten involved.

"Then there's Dad," she continued. "He's been sad too. I kept telling myself he was better, and he's improved since Mom's funeral. But when I saw him with Catherine—"

When she pressed her hand against her mouth, he dug his fingers into his knees. "It was like that for Mom when she met Ryan. Even at fifteen, I recognized it."

"I think new friendships give them hope. They see life is going to get better. We need hope." Her hands covered his. "You reminded me how important hope is. Thank you for your wisdom."

His chest puffed up, and then a thought clicked into place. What was she really saying? There was more than a thank-you. Yes, he knew about hope because he'd been in a place without it. Made it his mission to offer hope.

"I've devoted my life to helping others," he started, searching for the words to explain without divulging his secret.

"But I need to work out this problem with my brother in my own time. I've told you my plan." Heat flooded his cheeks. He hadn't meant to be abrupt. But he'd just found her, found this... this feeling. He wasn't going to jeopardize it because of his past.

What would she say if he told her he'd been silent when his brother had suffered a concussion? Would she look at him with respect and admiration or disgust? Would she despise him when she learned he hadn't rallied his family to stop Whit from going pro?

Gentle hands on his face brought him to the present. "Hey."

He swallowed. *Tell her*. She'd talked about hope. Maybe there was hope she could forgive him.

"I still have regrets about Mom and Robin," she said. "If I can shelter you from those...your family clearly loves you. They drove here just to ask you to attend the shower. Don't take them for granted."

She blinked hard. Was she crying?

Before he could reach for her, she stood. "I have a super craving for chocolate. Where is the hospital cake when you need it?"

The truth filled his throat, but he didn't speak. She deserved his honesty. He'd have to come clean. She was nudging him; he got that. At least she pushed and then backed off, gave him space to think.

When he stood, she studied the floor.

"You're amazing." They weren't the right words, the words he needed to say. But they were important too. He'd say the others soon, but for now, he needed to acknowledge her patience, her understanding.

She looked up, an interesting light in her eyes, and her lips slightly bent upward. "I thought I was pretty good at reading people until you came along."

When she glanced away, fear snaked through him.

"What? Did you make a wrong assumption about me again?"

If his heart didn't slow, he'd blow a vessel. Did she already know? She'd talked with Talley. But Whit and Talley ignored his failure. He hadn't earned their forgiveness. That was the worrisome part. The forgiveness he needed couldn't be earned.

"Sometimes a gal must follow her heart."

He swallowed his fear. Sometimes a man kept his mouth shut.

When she held out her hand, he took it.

CHAPTER EIGHTEEN

When Dana's heart slowed, and she managed to control her gasps, her thoughts finally chugged into gear. Wow! She blinked. Above her, Kyle's sweat-glistened shoulders heaved.

"Maybe we're getting too old for bedroom gymnastics."

He cocked his head just enough for one dark eye to narrow on her. "Direct shot to the ego."

A giggle sneaked past her dry lips. "Just saying."

When he squeezed onto his side, the mattress creaked and leaned toward the floor. However, his dark chest hair, growing in a horizontal T and arrowing beneath Sam's baseball sheets, claimed her attention—for two seconds. Heavens, she'd have to strip and wash Sam's bed. Should she vacuum the floor?

Untangling from the sheet, Dana rolled out of bed and slipped into her nightshirt covered with kittens. Wow! Was she the woman who mentioned disappointment? *Think again, girlfriend.* Disappointment would unfold if her assumptions about Kyle reconciling his family differences didn't play out. She pushed her still damp hair away from her face. It had to.

Her stomach churned. Time for a heart-to-heart with the man who'd just invaded hers. "I need a midnight snack." And a lot of assurances.

She chucked a pillow his way, but the playful toss didn't ease the tension tightening her muscles. What was wrong with her? Sam depended on her thoughtful decisions. Yet she lost her heart and then gave him her body. What happened if he didn't follow through?

He would. He was an intelligent, intentional man, and he'd promised her it would be resolved. If she couldn't trust his word, they had no relationship. Kyle had to come through for her and Sam. Otherwise, she'd exposed her family and her heart to a world of trouble.

He followed her to the kitchen, wearing only his boxers. "Sexy pj's."

"Sam picked this out for me." She pulled open the refrigerator door. "She's still lobbying for a pet."

"Every kid needs a pet."

She stopped and wagged her mean-mommy finger at him. "Do not encourage her. I have a vacation and an impending move in the future. I can't manage a kitten."

Kyle ran his thumb and forefinger across his mouth. "My lips are sealed. Just saying, we had a black lab when I was a kid. Toby was a great dog."

She pulled open the refrigerator door. "I hope you aren't a picky eater. I haven't shopped this week."

Kyle peeked over her shoulder, his breath warm on her neck. "Did I imagine a beautiful woman in a big hat promising blueberry pancakes?"

"For breakfast. I don't have enough for a midnight snack *and* breakfast."

"Mom used to have pancake night." His body heat continued to warm her back. "We loved it."

An image of the Murphy table, surrounded with eager

young faces, flashed in her head. She'd fantasized about Sunday dinners with her parents and Robin's family. The accident had robbed her of those anticipated family meals, but not Kyle. He had the relationships she craved, wanted for Sam. She'd witnessed a few members of his loving family, and they'd included her and Sam in their circle. Even Dad felt the Murphy family's love.

But it wasn't only Kyle's family that clutched her heart. She craved him, his intellect, his ambition, his presence, and the low cadence of his voice. She buried the images deep in her heart and scanned the refrigerator's lean contents.

"It's one of Sam's favorite meals too."

She rummaged through the bottles lining the refrigerator door, her fingers shaking along with her thoughts. "Chips and salsa? Plus, ..." She extracted two longnecks. "Beer."

"Perfect." He took the bottles from her and followed her to the area rug in front of the futon.

The word *perfect* circled her thoughts. After retrieving two worn cushions, she set the bowl of chips and salsa on the floor for their carpet picnic. Kyle, comfortable in his lack of apparel, stretched out on the floor, his head propped beneath one hand. He dredged a chip through the salsa and popped it into his mouth. Dana sipped her beer while discreetly following his gaze to his windbreaker draped carelessly across her sofa. A white envelope peeked from the side pocket.

"Sam was excited about the aquarium." She pressed a napkin to her lips. "I took her to the one in Atlanta, but I didn't know North Carolina had one."

"Mom took us a few times." Kyle's gaze remained locked on the envelope. "It's small and inexpensive, but we always had fun."

She hesitated before biting into a chip. "I used to love to go places with Robin. When you have siblings, you're never alone."

"And there's always an argument," Kyle added, but his comment seemed like an after-thought. Like his thoughts were somewhere else. He took a long swallow of beer, then pushed to his feet and retrieved the envelope.

"Is that from Whit?" she asked.

"Probably. I didn't see him slip it in my pocket. But that's in character for him—or Talley."

When she bit into a chip, the crunch echoed. "I can give you a moment if you need privacy."

"That's not necessary." He sipped his beer, spinning the letter on the coffee table with his index finger.

The refrigerator hummed through the silence. After a few cycles, Kyle set his bottle on the table and fingered the envelope. He huffed out a breath and opened the flap. A photo dropped to the floor.

"Never fails." Kyle turned over the photo of a building with a For Sale sign in front of it and stuffed it back into the envelope.

"Is everything okay?"

"Yes."

But it wasn't. The lusty man who shared her bed thirty minutes ago had tensed beside her.

"Do you want to talk about it?"

Kyle tossed the card toward his jacket, and it fluttered to the ground.

"That." He jerked his thumb toward the envelope. "Is the reason I avoid him."

She folded her hand over his until he relaxed his fist and interlaced his fingers with hers.

He huffed out a breath and shot her a half-hearted smile. "I didn't mean to direct my family drama on you. My brother has a knack for flipping my switch."

"Robin knew how to do that too. I miss those petty arguments. With Robin, an argument was like a test. You know how it is with the little sister?" Except maybe he didn't. Maybe it cramped his style since he was the oldest, and the roles were reversed. Robin was always in charge, always the star. Dana still missed her something fierce.

"If I got an unexpected outcome from one of Robin's so-called tests, I knew what to avoid with friends and acquaintances. She had to forgive me. We were sisters."

A shadow crossed Kyle's features. What the heck? Had she caused the distance in his stare? His cheek twitched.

"It's kind of sweet that he wants you to move closer," she said.

Kyle's features crumpled into an incredulous expression. "Sweet? You declined your dad's offer to help with a down payment on a house. My brother wants to *buy* my office building for me."

He had a point. There were always two sides to consider. Dad was trying to help her and Sam. But Whit's actions were condescending. Robin would've lost her mind if Dana had given her coaching advice. Why was it easy to hurt the people you loved?

"You're right. I only have an undergrad in nursing. But I'm a competent woman who can purchase a home for me and Sam. You've gone through medical school and literally have the lives of others in your hands. Having your little brother try to purchase your practice for you kind of undermines everything you've worked for and attained."

Kyle also had a point about her rejection of Dad's help. Self-confidence was an admirable trait. Pride? Pride was often a double-edged sword. She needed to talk to Dad again. Make sure her motivations were true.

And Kyle? Had she minimized the rift with his brother because she yearned for his big family? What if she'd made a mistake? Maybe what she'd seen was an act for outsiders. If so, it had worked. But what could separate him not only from his brother but also from his entire family? She only knew one thing that would resurrect such a reaction: guilt stemming from fear.

She moved closer. "I don't understand everything you're feeling, but I'll help any way I can. If you'll let me."

"Thanks."

He didn't look away from the envelope. Okay, so he didn't want her help. He'd given her nonverbal clues in that direction for over three weeks. She pushed the chips aside. Too bad. Grahams didn't give up. If so, she'd still be wallowing in grief. She couldn't sit by and let someone she cared about wallow in...guilt, anger? Who knew? It better not be ego.

She squared her shoulders. "When I was eight months pregnant with Sam, a two-hour car ride was a big deal. Talley traveled over three to ask you to come to the shower. Your family seemed happy to see you." She swallowed. "You seemed happy to see them too."

She glided her fingers through his coarse dark hair. The bleak look in his dark eyes tugged at her heart.

"Talley and Whit are a good match. They'll be awesome parents." He shrugged. "Seeing them... made me a little sappy."

And made her want to get closer to him. "You are very fortunate to have such a loving family. They are a special life gift."

When he opened his arms, she snuggled against his side. She didn't want to argue or nag. She just wanted to make his life better. Hadn't he asked her to do that?

He rested his face against her head, and she tightened her hold on him, matching her breaths, so her chest rose and fell with his.

"It's not them," he said. "It's me. What I can't forget."

"Maybe it's closer to what you can't forgive," she guessed.

When he stiffened, she held tight. She'd answered with her heart without thought to how he would take it.

"Sorry. I needed to say that for me." She searched his features for understanding. "But maybe my mistakes will help you work through your family issues."

"Maybe," he said. But there was a slight catch in his speech.

Why was love hard? "I still struggle with my decision to stop Mom's life support," she said after a deep breath. "Not because it was wrong. Because it was hard for Dad. He hasn't been the same since. Until today."

Kyle pulled her against him, cradling her hands close to his heart. Its rhythmic beat soothed and slowed her breaths. They might not agree on therapy, but on family and love? Sam needed family and love, and so did she. If Kyle couldn't provide that—

She squeezed her eyes closed, suppressing the tear buildup. Sam came first regardless of the fallout to her heart.

"You told me you strive to give every patient hope." She hesitated, her heart thundering in her chest. "I need hope too."

He stilled behind her. When his grip loosened, she turned in his arms, cradling his long healing hands in hers. His brow furrowed, his dark eyes blazing with intensity.

"I want a big loving network for Sam, and for me. But I also want you."

When he glanced up, a shudder ripped through her. "My family will love you and Sam."

"And the shower?"

"I'll go with you and your family," he whispered.

"No last-minute excuses?" *Shut up, Dana!* She couldn't. Her decisions had cost Sam her father. Perhaps a grandmother and aunt. What if they cost her this man?

When she cupped his jaw in her palms, his stubble tickled her flesh.

"You're asking for a lot," he said.

"More like demanding." A tear spilled from the corner of her eye. "It's not fair, demanding compensation for what I failed to give my daughter. But I've got to do it anyway."

A sad smile curved his mouth. "It's a motherly requirement."

She nodded, not trusting her voice.

DANA BLINKED at the sunlight streaming through Sam's bedroom window the following morning. Cool air brushed her back where Kyle's warm body had been. She raised to one elbow to view the bug-eyed frog with a clock inside its belly. 10:30 A.M.

Holy cow, she hadn't just slept. She'd been in a coma.

A note tucked beneath the alarm clock fluttered from the overhead fan.

CINDERELLA, or maybe I should call you Sleeping Beauty. Making early rounds. I'll take a rain check on the blueberry pancakes. Text me when you awaken.

Kyle

KYLE? Dana grabbed her cell. They made love twice, and he signed his name? Dana jabbed Send and stomped to the bathroom. What did she expect, *Love, Kyle* with a few x's and o's? Her giggle came out more like a grunt. At least he'd left a note. She adjusted the shower temperature and stepped into the tub. Plus, they had a date to pick up Sam. She hoped her little one enjoyed the night as much as she had.

Thirty minutes later, the front door rattled. Dad poked his head inside the door. "Good morning."

Mortified by the heat singeing her cheeks, Dana placed bread in the toaster. She was a consenting adult, for Pete's sake. Dad didn't judge her.

"Morning. Do you want a piece of toast?"

"No, thanks. Catherine and I ate an early breakfast."

Pain speared through her jaw at the quick jerk of her head. Now, who was judging? But it was her dad. "She seemed like a nice lady." And she was not fooling Dad with her lame nonchalance.

"She is." Dad sat in a dining room chair. "So, how was your evening with Kyle?"

How the heck did she answer his question? He's awesome in bed, Dad. Dana huffed out a breath. Throw out the toaster. Her cheeks could brown bread. Nope, her cheeks could heat the kitchen in January.

He held up his cup for her to top off his coffee. "Thanks. I'll meet Whit and pick up Sam if you want to catch an extra shift this evening."

The toast popped up, hiding her sigh of relief. "I was proud of her kindness with Noel."

"She's a special girl, just like her mother."

His kind words cracked her remnants of annoyance like nutmeat from a shell. "Thanks, Dad. I had excellent parenting."

She peeled away the crust from her toast. "I kind of made an executive decision for us."

Dad looked up, his gaze steady and interested.

"We're going to Talley's shower." The words tumbled from her mouth in a rapid torrent, but she might as well get to the heart of the matter. Dad loved and supported her. She could talk to him, and there was no better time than the present.

"Did you talk Kyle into attending?"

That was the plan. No, that was her line in the sand. She couldn't believe she'd drawn it, but there was no other way—not for her and Sam. Someday, when she couldn't distinguish Kyle's scent everywhere, she'd give Dad the details. Not today, so she nodded.

"I told Catherine you'd see the way of it."

"I'm sorry?"

"Life's too short to let petty issues separate you from the ones you love." He peered over his glasses at her. "Isn't that your line?"

She nodded again, feeling like one of Sam's bobbleheads.

"Catherine lost her husband. It was his health, not an accident. She was a good person to talk to. Things..." He drained the last of his beverage. "I've been avoiding something."

A bite of toast caught in Dana's throat. She sipped her juice, and a chill lifted the fine hairs on her forearms.

When Dad squeezed her arm, moisture brightened his eyes. "I never thanked you for helping me make the right decision about your mother."

"None needed." Air moved through her throat like glass, adding a brittle sound to her words.

"It's what your mother would've wanted. I'm ashamed I left the decision on your shoulders because I couldn't let her go."

"I'm glad I was there to help you with it. It's just—"

"Life's too short." He pointed at the sampler framed on her wall. *Say it. Do it. Be it.*

Dana drew a steadying breath to ease the clench in her chest. "Mom didn't have a domestic bone in her body. She'd laugh if she knew I hung her gift in the kitchen."

"She probably bought it at a sports charity event," Dad said. "Be glad it's not a T-shirt."

"It's one of the few things I moved from Blowing Rock. Every time I look at it, I hear her words in my head."

"Good words for a basketball coach and a top-notch oncology nurse."

He could always bring a smile to her lips. "Thanks for telling me."

"I'm sorry I let you down."

How many times had he held her, protected her, made her feel safe? He'd paid for her education, and that education had enabled her to make an informed decision. She stood and wrapped her arms around his neck. His once-thick dark hair had thinned, along with his shoulders, but he was still her rock.

"You've helped me become the person I am today. I help people. I give them the information they need to make informed decisions about their loved ones."

"I'm proud of you." He patted her hand.

"Thanks. And thanks for telling me. I felt it was the right decision for Mom and for you, me, and Sam. Even with that knowledge..."

He stood and cupped her chin in his hands the same way he'd done when she was little, and he was the biggest man in her universe. "Never doubt your decision. I should've told you months ago."

"You told me today."

"Only because of something Catherine said last night."

"It's interesting how the universe puts people in your path at the right time." She raked the toast crumbs into a pile with her fingers. "Did Catherine mention the problem between Kyle and Whit?"

Dad shook his head. "According to Murphy legend, the fallout occurred around the time of Whit's marriage to Talley. The family wants them to resolve it."

"Kyle can be stubborn."

Dad chuckled. "Like someone else I know?"

"I gave him an ultimatum."

Dad straightened. "Oookaaay."

"He promised to resolve the issue. He's let it continue too long. We lost Mom and Robin in one moment. That could happen to Kyle."

Dad's distant gaze haunted her. Was he remembering the night of the accident? She'd just put Sam down and was preparing to study for a test. One moment, they were a close family. The next minute, half of them had been taken.

"What if Kyle received a similar call about Whit?" She rolled her lips to keep the emotions at bay. "There were no bad feelings between me and Mom and Robin, and I still worry about the last time I said 'I love you,' or 'I'm proud of you.' I hope they knew how much I loved them."

Dad stared at his empty cup. "They knew. But I see your point about Kyle."

"If he can't mend the breach in his family, he can't be a role model for Sam. We deserve more."

"Sounds like something your mother would say. She was proud of you when you chose nursing."

"Really? I always felt like I let her down. She spent hours trying to teach me basketball, volleyball, and softball. I was a disaster."

"You were with sports. But only because your path led to nursing. Your mom worried she'd let you down. To be honest, I felt like she let Robin down because she was busy teaching you. Although Robin didn't need help with sports, she still needed her mother's love."

Dana blinked. "I've never thought about our lives from their perspective."

"Kids always want to please." He shook his finger at her. "It's our fault if you didn't know how proud we were of you. That's why I overcompensate with Sam."

"Grandkids are a second chance to get it right."

A big smile replaced his sober expression. "Sam's a dandy." He glanced at the wall clock ticking over the sink. "Better get on the road. I don't want to hold up Whit and Talley. It makes me nervous when a pregnant woman goes on the road."

Dana waved him goodbye and closed the cottage door. Out of habit, she picked up the marker suspended by her wall calendar and marked off another day. Three shifts and she'd attain her goal. Maybe it was time to call a realtor because she'd almost won.

Dana froze. Won? How had she turned her aspiration to purchase a home for Sam into a competition with Kyle? She'd resented Mom and Robin's competitive natures for years because she'd felt inadequate. But she didn't feel inadequate now.

Dad was right. She'd found nursing, and she was good at her job, good with people. Mom hadn't cared about her choice. Her mother had just wanted her to find what made her happy. Why hadn't she seen that?

Why didn't Kyle see time with his family was more important than money? Why was she working so hard to prove she could provide a home for Sam? They had a home. Dad wouldn't be with them forever. They needed to enjoy the closeness they shared. She'd been blind. Pushing Kyle to finish so he'd resolve his family issues while she'd been doing the same thing.

She didn't need more shifts. She needed time with her family. Maybe Kyle's secret wound prevented him from seeing the path to freedom, but it hadn't blinded her. Time to put her money where her mouth was.

CHAPTER NINETEEN

K yle raked through his shirts the morning of the baby shower. Why did he agree to go? He'd developed a plan. Attending the shower before he had the payment wasn't it. Still, he'd promised Dana he'd go—no excuses. Sometimes he was a fool.

His luck, Whit had already researched appointing his clinic. His phone alerted from the scarred chest in his bedroom. Probably Dana. If he didn't leave in the next twenty-five minutes, he'd be late.

He jerked on a blue plaid button-down. If he hadn't promised her, he could've gotten in an extra ED shift. Family drama was a pain. A man couldn't find peace with so many family members residing in the same state. On that, he and Dana needed to agree to disagree.

Although he was still working on his touchy-feely skills, he was improving. Dana meant well but losing her mother and sister in an accident distorted her perspective. Whit wasn't going anywhere. In another month, Kyle would put a fat check in Whit's hand, and his debt would be paid in full. He'd be his own man.

They could relocate anywhere. Dana would probably want to stay near her dad, which was okay. He liked George Graham. Good thing. If things continued to progress, George would be his father-in-law.

When his phone signaled again, he stopped buttoning his shirt and tapped the screen. The memory of Dana's spicy scent filled his mind. Since Whit had booked the Old Sunberry Hotel for the shower, maybe he could sneak into Dana's room tonight. There were plenty of kids in the Murphy tribe so Sam would be thoroughly entertained. He could go for another evening with just the two of them.

His phone buzzed a third time. Maybe Dana wanted him to pick up something on the way. The name of one of his patients blinked on the display.

"It's a patient, Dana," he muttered.

She'd be disappointed, but he'd taken an oath. She'd understand his patients came first. As for Whit and his family, he'd make it up to them when he went home with the check.

Within minutes, he'd added a tie and a laundered lab coat to his attire, tossed the Subaru's keys on the chest, and pushed his bike outside. The cool breeze brushed his face, solidifying his decision. What if Dana didn't get over it?

When he arrived at the hospital, Kyle clicked his bike lock into place. He issued a text to his ED colleague and another to the clinic about meeting his patient. Dana would be worried. Sam was probably making her crazy, but she'd forget about Kyle's absence the minute the Murphy kids and friends surrounded her. When he was a kid, he loved family get-togethers.

He slipped into an empty exam room and pressed Dana's contact.

"Kyle?"

"Something's come up."

"Are you on your way? If we don't leave soon, we'll be late. Sam is about to drive me nuts. She can't wait to see Noel and Whit."

"I'm at Wilcox, waiting on a patient." Kyle held his breath.

A tapping sounded outside the exam room door, and a nurse peeked in. "Your patient is here," she whispered.

Kyle nodded. If he didn't finish the conversation with Dana, she'd really be ticked.

"Did I lose you?" he said.

"I'm here."

Boy, was she ever. Her brittle tone sounded more like ice clinking in a glass.

"Go on without me. I'll see what's going on with Hobbs. If it's minor, I'll follow you there."

"So, I'll let your family know you're coming but will be a little late?" she pressed.

Kyle grimaced. The exam would only take thirty minutes. He could leave in an hour or two. "I'll text you an update as soon as I'm finished. I'm sure it's minor."

"You aren't on call."

"Says the nurse coaching me on empathy," he said.

Silence. Okay, she didn't find his humor funny.

"If I don't see Hobbs, the physician on call will send him to the ED. He'd have a long wait, and they'd page me anyway."

"They'd page the oncologist on call."

Kyle forced a deep breath. It was a shower. Most guys didn't attend them. Why was it such a big deal to her?

"Drive safe," he said. "I'll text a status when I complete the exam."

At 11:30, he sent the first update to Dana.

. . .

KYLE: Waited for labs and sent Hobbs home with a script. Stayed for Sommer's discharge celebration. Sneaked one of your special bags from your locker. Sommers wheeled out with a big smile on her face.

Miss you.

HE HELD HIS BREATH, waiting for her response. She was probably still driving but should be pulling into Sunberry anytime.

KYLE: Making a quick round on 6-West and then heading home to change.

See you soon.

KYLE PUNCHED the elevator button for 6-West. Since he was in the building, it wouldn't take long to check on his patients. Dana already expected him to be late. Another thirty minutes wouldn't matter. He ran his index finger along his shirt collar. So, he was procrastinating. He understood Dana's priorities, and he'd made strides to align his with hers. He didn't take his family for granted. He, Whit, and Nate had shared some great times, and he was grateful they had his back.

But he hadn't had Whit's back. He'd failed his brother, failed his father's expectations. And he'd put that behind him after a few more ED shifts. Man, he couldn't wait to hand his brother a check.

The elevator shuddered to a halt, and he hurried over the threshold. Even with the cool air filtering the hall, the claustrophobia lingered. Stupid elevators. He'd never cared for them.

When Kyle finished the note on the last patient, he

stretched. Man, he was starving. His gaze rose to the wall clock above the unit desk. "Dana's going to be mad."

His phone screen, with its photo of his arm around Mr. Harris's shoulders, mocked him. Harris had sacrificed his health for his granddaughter's game. There were no guarantees in life. But it wasn't like he was waiting forever. He'd have the money in a few weeks.

He was missing a shower. It wasn't like the baby was attending. Showers were more for women, anyway. By the time he biked home, changed, and drove to Sunberry, the festivities would be over. Besides, he didn't want a family audience when he told Whit what was on his mind. Worse, he wouldn't have the complete payment. He couldn't imagine giving his planned speech without the money. That would be like giving a patient chemo without anti-nausea medication.

So, what did he tell Dana?

He shoved his phone into his pocket. The ride home would clear his head. Once she returned from Sunberry, he'd fess up about his failure with his brother and hope she still respected him. He loved her, and he didn't want to start out a marriage with secrets. Marriage?

The bike bumped from the steel rack. How would that play out in a text? Sorry I stood you up to meet my parents, but would you marry me? He checked his side-view mirror and waved at the waiting motorist. The shower wasn't a meet-the-parents deal; it was a placate-his-lover deal. She'd kind of forced it on him. And he had meant to comply. Stuff happened.

Like falling in love. Man, they had a lot to talk about. Too bad he'd made her mad. He'd have to grovel, but Mom always said the one you loved was worth the effort. At the stoplight, he checked his texts.

· · ·

DANA: Sam loves your family. The kids are having a blast and so cute. Hurry. You're missing out!

BELOW HER TEXT a video of Sam and Noel dancing together played. Kyle laughed and pushed away from the curb. Soon, that adorable girl would be his daughter. He'd have to chat with Sam about marrying her mother. Ryan had talked with Kyle and his brothers before asking their mom to marry him.. Of course, they'd been older, but he wanted Sam to understand her opinions were important. Man, he had a lot to discuss with his future wife—after she got over being mad at him. Maybe he should go shopping before she returned. Nothing he hated more. But Dana was worth it, and he'd need an olive branch.

The rock flashed in his peripheral vision. He gripped the handlebars to correct the sudden crank of his wheel.

CHAPTER TWENTY

He wasn't coming.

Dana fidgeted in the ivory wing chair lining the Sunberry Hotel's dance floor. The artfully restored hotel created the perfect venue for the Murphy-friends-and-family gathering, where Dana fell in the shadowed background between friends and family. She'd been welcomed, included.

Noel and Sam, along with two little boys and another girl, had converted the space into their personal gymnasium. Dad and Catherine mingled and laughed. Dana had given the ridiculous Kyle updates and received sympathetic nods. Everyone knew he wasn't coming.

Although the buzzing of her phone continued from inside her leather bag, she didn't reach for it. Her last tolerant gene had left the building. Besides, she refused to type what she was thinking. No, no, no. The words circling her brain like a flock of vultures could not be documented. Their impending breakup was pitiful enough without adding another excuse to his tally.

"Message received," she muttered.

Pride and ego motivated Kyle. She'd foolishly believed she

could change him, or better, fix him. His family had been unable to diminish his flaws, and ego and pride were definite flaws. But she'd been determined to try. Some flaws, like some conditions, couldn't be treated.

She swallowed the lump of sadness forming in her throat and forced her lips to curve upward.

She should have known. Should have recognized the knowing look in Whit's gaze when she explained Kyle had been delayed and would join them later. Kyle's brother had known, or at least suspected. Like her, sadness, not anger, filled his heart.

How could such a brilliant physician be blind? Maybe Kyle didn't need the one thing she craved. Maybe he was merely taking the path of least resistance. Or were she and Sam a substitute for the family he'd estranged? It wasn't like he had a big hole to fill during his limited downtime from work. She understood his dedication to his patients, but she would not condone his family abandonment. How did she know he wouldn't abandon her and Sam in the future?

Across the expansive room, Dad caught her eye. He'd regained the cheerful nature with Catherine that had been such a big part of his character, a part missing since the loss of Mom and Robin. At least there was something positive about her attendance. Plus, she'd met new friends too. Except it would be awkward to continue a relationship in Sunberry once she broke it off with Kyle.

To Dana's right, Catherine pressed a phone to her ear and stared at her. Once Dana found a suitable home, Catherine could use the cottage for visits. Unless—

Heat raced across her cheeks. She wasn't going there. Not about Dad. But if Dad and Catherine—well, it would be awkward. Not that she planned to stay in touch with Kyle. Except for work. Yep, it would be awkward—until he started dating another hospital colleague.

When Dad and Catherine approached her, she stood. "Are you about ready to head back to Raleigh?"

Catherine tucked her phone back in her purse. "Kyle called me. He's on the road here. He asked me to tell you not to leave until he arrived."

"I'm sorry he involved you," Dana said. "But I'm working tomorrow. I need to get Sam home, feed her, and get her into bed."

"He'll be here in an hour," Catherine said. "He also asked me to ask the rest of the family to wait here."

A flutter of hope lifted her thoughts. "Maybe he's finally going to address what's been eating at him." Dana blinked hard. "I hope he does. But I'm not family." She'd wanted to be, still admired the Murphy family. Maybe someday, she'd create a family like it, like what she had before the accident.

"Are you working another overtime shift?" Dad asked.

Which was strange. Dad rarely commented about her additional shifts. He understood she was nearing her goal. Still, the smile she noted earlier had dissolved into deep grooves bracketing his mouth.

"Only three more to go." Her tone came out flat, like the emotion claiming her belly. She'd gone online yesterday and checked out Disney hotel rooms. It would be cool to stay in the park, and they were advertising discounts. Sam had been patient, and Dana could afford to spend more for a cute room with her favorite character over the bed.

"Sam's having a great time, and we have the space until seven." Catherine's voice was gentle but persuasive.

"I thought the shower ended at three thirty," Dana said.

"It does." Catherine glanced at Dad. "But we're having a private dinner for our family and yours."

She got where this was going. Kyle wasn't going to manipulate her into staying. Enough was enough. She'd been clear. He'd known.

Talley and Whit joined them.

"Any idea what's going on with Kyle?" Whit asked.

Dana lifted her hands. "None." Furthermore, she didn't want to know—much.

"But you're going to stay?" Talley took Dana's hands in her warm palms. "I know it's a big ask, and he's been a jerk—"

"Got that right," Whit muttered.

Talley pivoted toward her husband and fisted her hands against her sides, which emphasized her baby bump. "Climb down off your white horse. We had a hard time getting through to you too." She turned to Dana, her expressive features bright. "Murphy men can be real jerks, but they come around nicely *if* you stand your ground. That said, they are so... stubborn."

Talley scrunched up her face and spit out her tongue. On another day, Dana might've laughed.

"I promise I'll personally hold Kyle down so you can make your point," Talley said. "I just want us to be a family again. Like I said before, I'm not above begging."

Just the thought of such a generous woman groveling because of something her boyfriend—Dana shook her head to clear the aberrant thought—something Kyle had done aggravated her very last nerve. Plus, it was embarrassing. Where had her brain been when she'd vowed to make him see the light with his family? The reminder of her righteous plan sent a shudder through her.

Grahams pulled through. At least that had been Mom's motto. That said, Mom's euphemisms ran at fifty percent. That one had been a keeper.

"We'll stay for the dinner because you've been such a lovely host and hostess," Dana said. "But Kyle has burned through his final do-over with me."

"That's too bad," Talley said. "I could really use a great

sister-in-law with all this testosterone invading the Murphy space."

Although Dana wanted to befriend Talley, a relationship with her would be too awkward. After today, she wanted to limit reminders of Kyle. Tears and hissy fits weren't her style, especially in front of Kyle's family and Sam. However, sitting in the closet, sucking her kneecaps, had some appeal. Heartache required privacy.

She stayed busy, helping the family disassemble shower decorations. Whit hovered, though Talley had the energy of three pregnant ladies.

She swallowed the sudden lump of emotion. Why had she allowed fantasies of creating sister bonds and cousin's birthdays to continue? Shaking off her blues, she pasted a smile on her face and boxed up the last of the shower gifts for Whit and Nate to haul to the car.

At 4:10, Dana tapped her phone, ignoring the multiple text messages and voice mail from Kyle. She was leaving as soon as Sam finished dinner. It wouldn't surprise her if Kyle didn't show.

When the caterer completed preparations, the family moved toward the large table decorated with vases of brilliant pink peonies from the shower. Nate hauled in a small table for the children and placed it adjacent to the adult's table. Kyle's mother, Ava, and Catherine served the kids. Dana doubted Sam would eat the chicken nuggets, fries, and fruit cups provided for the children. Still, her daughter's constant giggle rang through the group. Too bad adults rarely modeled children.

Although Talley invited Dana to sit near her and Whit, she declined and sat at the opposite end near Dad and Catherine. Besides, the children's table was closer to her end, and it seemed fair for her to help with additional servings for the kids while Talley and the other Murphy women enjoyed downtime.

By five thirty, the servers removed the entrée flatware and served apple cobbler with big scoops of vanilla ice cream that filled the area with the homey scent of cinnamon and apples. The kids enjoyed leftover cupcakes from the shower.

Dana leaned toward Dad, lowering her voice. "As soon as dessert is complete, we need to leave."

He nodded, although the corners of his mouth drooped. The clink of glassware and the scrape of utensils cut through the low murmur of voices. Dana wasn't the only one hiding her disappointment. Kyle's continued absence had subdued the boisterous Murphy clan.

They'd waited and hoped. But, once again, the eldest sibling disappointed them.

At the end of the long table, Whit stood. "I just wanted to extend Talley's and my gratitude for sharing the celebration of the next generation of Murphys. My wife had the good sense to add a little girl to this group of Murphy men."

"I pity her boyfriends," Hope added, and the family laughed.

When a door closed and the linen fluttered, Dana turned toward the exit.

Kyle, dressed in his usual blue oxford shirt and starched jeans, limped toward the head of the long table and Whit. A bandage covered his forehead above his discolored cheek and right eye.

"Sorry, family." He found her gaze and held. "I ran into a few obstacles getting here. But thanks for coming and waiting for me."

When he glanced at his shoes and rolled his lips, the back of Dana's throat swelled. Whatever was coming next required courage.

"Pride runs thick in my veins, thanks to Ryan, Mom, and

the rest of you. Anyway, I love all of you and have missed arguing with you."

Laughter rippled through the room, and many family members wiped at their eyes. Kyle's gaze moved from face to face. "I stayed away too long. But I'm home now, and I plan to stay here." His gaze bored into hers. "If my plan works out."

Plan? Dana blinked. What plan? They hadn't made *plans*. He'd made a promise, which he'd broken, for the most part.

He turned to Whit and pulled an envelope from his pocket. "I've been saving to pay you back for my education. But I figured that would tick you off. Anyway, it's not money. It's a contract on the property you sent to me. The place is perfect for my oncology practice, just like you said." He shrugged. "I'm not the only one in the Murphy family with spectacular ideas."

"Whoa!" Nate raised his glass. "Somebody, record this. My big brother just admitted the rest of us have good ideas too. Bravo, bro. That must have been painful."

"Thank you, Nate, for your insights." Kyle turned to Whit. "I ignored the risks you took to play in the NFL. That's something I'll have to live with. I failed my promise to Dad to keep you guys safe. I was supposed to take care of you." He looked around the table. "All of you. I broke that promise."

Whit stood. "You weren't responsible for my decision."

"You're right. But I should've worked harder at talking you out of getting beat up for a living." Kyle hugged his brother. Sniffling filled the silence while they embraced and clapped one another on the back.

When Whit stepped back, Kyle continued. "I spent thirty minutes laying out the purchase details on the drive here. Wouldn't you know, it wasn't ready when I arrived?"

"Oh." Ava pressed her napkin to her lips but didn't try to hide the joyful tears filling her eyes.

"But I want a promise from you too." Kyle wagged his finger at Whit. "Back off with the financial support. Give me a chance to save face, especially in front of the woman I love."

Dana froze. He did *not* just announce he loved her in front of Dad, Sam, and his family. Kyle merely grinned at her and turned to Talley. Dana huffed out a breath. No, sir, Kyle Murphy. He could not launch a bomb into her life and then move on like it wasn't a big deal. He'd humiliated her, betrayed her, and, and then professed to love her? Nuh-uh. This wasn't happening. But her jerky boyfriend was motioning for Talley to stand.

With a blush on her cheeks, Talley stood by his side. When he leaned forward, Dana assumed he was going to hug his sister-in-law. Instead, he whispered in her ear.

Whit frowned.

"Stand down, little brother. She gave me permission to touch." Kyle kneeled and pressed his hand to Talley's abdomen.

"Little Murphy Princess, I promise to be the best uncle ever. I'll be a phone call away when you need the voice of reason to stop your dad from flattening your latest boyfriend. I promise you can stay with me when Mom and Dad need adult time. I'll step in to help you with your bike or teach you to drive. I'd offer tutoring services, but your mom has that covered."

After another round of family hugs and slaps on the back, Kyle moved toward Dana, his gaze never leaving hers. "I'm sorry I wasn't here to introduce you to the love of my life, Dana Graham. I've disappointed her, and she deserves a far better man than me.

"She took me on as a project, and I was a serious work in

progress. But she made me a better physician, a better brother, and a better man. I'm sure all of you sold her on the Murphy family. I just hope she won't quit on me because I can't imagine life without her and her beautiful daughter in it."

He stopped in front of Dad. "Mr. Graham. With your permission and hers, I plan to steal your Cinderella."

Steal her? Dana didn't know what had injured his head, but it was going to be small compared to the unkind thoughts sweeping through her. Worse, Kyle had the audacity to walk past her chair. He knelt and whispered something to Sam. After Dana gave her daughter a reassuring smile, she roasted Kyle with her meanest glare. He ignored her.

"There's something for you in the lobby," he told Sam. "They wouldn't let me bring it into the dining area." He shrugged. "Rules."

Dana squeezed her bag so hard, something inside crunched. There was movement beside her, then Sam's whispered voice, and her dad's. She needed to get out of here, get away from the looks, especially the pleading in Kyle's intense gaze. Her feet felt rooted to the polished wooden floor. How dare he do this in front of his family. In front of Dad and Sam. This wasn't right. It broke her heart, but it wasn't right.

She pushed back from the table, relieved her muscles finally responded to her commands. Sweat tickled her face. Sounds expanded and contracted like a giant heart pounding in her mind. When her stomach rolled, she darted to the powder room. Inside the large room, decorated with burgundy flocked wallpaper and red tufted furniture, she leaned against the door, gasping for air.

He couldn't do this. Couldn't humiliate her in front of his family and then come riding in like some white knight to save the day. He'd never even said he loved her. Never mentioned uprooting her and Sam to move to Sunberry. He had denied wanting to return. All of it was lies. Maybe he'd lied to himself too, but she and Sam were collateral damage. How could she trust him with her life and her precious daughter's?

Her thoughts banged inside her skull like rocks in an empty can. Somehow, she had to collect Dad and Sam to return home. She needed the safety and comfort of her cottage, a place far from the Sunberry Hotel and Kyle.

On the other side of the heavy carved door, muffled voices sounded. Dana wiped at her eyes and hurried to the end stall. Pressing a piece of tissue to her lips, she waited.

Water ran in the sink. "I told you he'd make his way home."

"But it has been so long. I'd almost lost hope."

"Ava Murphy, you're the strongest woman I know. You know better than to give up."

"When he said he was moving home . . ." Ava blew her nose. "I thought my heart would burst with love. All the hurt and guilt churning inside me dissolved. He's my firstborn, Stella. He's coming home."

While the two women continued to talk about the prodigal Murphy son, Dana froze. Kyle had hurt his mother far more than he'd hurt her, yet she and his grandmother had forgiven him because they loved him. Dana blotted her tears. Where was her forgiveness? Where was her vow to make every day better for the people she loved? Yes, she suffered humiliation, hurt, and disappointment. Those emotions often accompanied love. So what was she going to do, wallow in self-pity or embrace the gifts life presented?

CHAPTER TWENTY-ONE

A lthough his bike wreck banged up his body, nothing hurt worse than the dreadful emptiness squeezing his chest. Kyle suppressed the groan from his mother's hug. Had he suffered a pneumothorax, or was it a side effect of Dana's stunned features? Her tortured stare was a long way from undying love.

"Love you," his mother whispered.

"Love you too."

His family milled around him, hugging and shaking his hand. Where was Dana? He needed to talk to her, just the two of them, but Mom was crying. He also put her through the wringer. He couldn't just blow her off and rush to Dana. Where the heck was Talley? She always had her female antennae in the air. He needed help distracting his family because if he didn't get to Dana soon, he might lose her.

At no time during his wild drive to Sunberry had he visualized a reaction like this.

"Guys." Whit's voice cut through the din.

"Thank you, brother," Kyle murmured, suppressing the urge to shake his fists in the air.

"We better give Kyle private time with Dana." Whit moved through his family members, clearing an exit path for Kyle. "It never goes well to blindside a woman with a declaration," Whit whispered.

Kyle nodded. He got it. He just hoped it wasn't too late.

Outside the hotel, the last shafts of sun peeked through the new foliage on the crape myrtles shading the streets. Panic arced through Kyle's bruised body. Where was she? He crossed Main Street to the park bordering the entrance to the Opera House. He'd resolved many problems on the iron benches nestled in the small park. Today, the outcome didn't look promising; the empty benches met his gaze.

No sign of a familiar yellow sundress. He turned on his good foot until he faced the hotel again. Nothing. It was like his hometown had swallowed her. Then, the flash of yellow fluttered in the entrance of the hotel. By the time he'd limped to the sidewalk, Dana had crossed Main Street to meet him.

She squinted at his bandage. "What happened to your face?"

The shaky quality of her voice cut into him. He'd hurt her again. Why couldn't he get this relationship thing right? He'd always been a smart guy—until it came to people.

He wanted to touch her, hug her close, but he held back while she sat on the bench, her arms folded protectively across her chest.

"Bike got away from me. Distracted rider."

Instead of grinning at his sad attempt at humor, she squinted at his head. He ran his hand through his hair and fingered the blood-crusted strands.

"I was in a hurry. Craig shot a few staples in my head, then I went home, changed clothes, and drove here." He was here to talk about his heart, not his head.

"No helmet?" She moved toward him, gently touched her fingers to his skin.

Then again, if his head injury meant touching him... "I was wearing one, but I guess it slid up. It's only a three-centimeter laceration."

"Did they check you for concussion? You shouldn't be operating a vehicle. How come they didn't clean it up?"

"Hey." He grabbed her fingers and pressed them close to his chest, forcing her to look at him and see he was serious.

"I was thinking some pretty hurtful things about you." She dropped her gaze. "It's terrible to lose people you love. But it's worse when you worry you didn't tell them how much they mean to you. I didn't want that to happen to you."

"It kind of did."

"Your dad was a Marine. He knew the risks," she said. "I bet he made sure you knew he loved you every time he had to leave."

"He did. I was talking about today. Your message came through loud and clear the moment I landed in the ditch."

She was frowning again. Dang, he wanted to see her sunny smile.

"Why were you in a ditch?"

"I never knew the power of a low-speed impact. I mean, I know the stats. But firsthand experience is worth a lot of words. I'll have to replace my bike. The jerk who hit me never stopped. Thank goodness Harris was home."

The color drained from Dana's cheeks. "Wait. Replay your last statement. A car... hit you?"

"That's my best guess. I haven't learned to fly, and the last thing I remember was moving through air. Next thing I knew, I was face down in the grass, which beats landing on the asphalt. Have you seen a bad case of road rash? It's nasty."

Her chin fell to her chest.

"Hey? Dana? I'm fine. But you were right." He tipped her chin upward to gaze into her amazing blue eyes. They were a bit glassy. "I get it. I mean, like crystal. I could've been gone.

But the people I left behind would always wonder, would shoulder guilt like I did with my dad."

"Fear makes us do crazy things," she whispered. "I wanted to push you away because I was afraid I'd get wrapped up in loving you and forget the gifts in my life. But I was already forgetting."

He shook his head. "You're fabulous. It's me who needed to come clean. You helped me see that. I was getting it, really. Change is hard. I kept making the same mistake. The answer was right in front of me. I couldn't reach out and grab it." He shrugged. "Until the bike flight."

When she narrowed her eyes, he lifted his hands. "Now, Dana. It is kind of funny."

She shook her head.

"No, really." He held up his thumb and index finger. "Just a little bit."

She straightened. "The accident was the only reason you came to Sunberry."

Aw, jeez. "I finally understood. Really. The accident forced me to reach out and take hold."

"Do you know how humiliating it was for me to make excuses to your family?"

"I was the jerk. My family knows that. That's why I asked them to wait."

Her features softened, but she wasn't ready to forgive him yet.

"I was done with you. This was the last straw. I told you I couldn't be with a man who disrespected his family. I meant it."

"And I couldn't live knowing I'd never make a family with you. I almost lost you." The words abrased his throat. "But love isn't a faucet we turn off and on."

She pulled away from him and placed her hands on her hips. "Okay, hotshot. Just how do you *know* your latest screwup didn't destroy my love? Because you are in the 'Serious Risk' category."

"You're passionate about what you believe is right, what is helpful for others. I understand and share your passion."

"But sometimes we get it wrong," she whispered.

"There is nothing—" Kyle pressed his forehead to hers. "Nothing you could do to make me stop loving you. I can't imagine a life without you in it."

When he released her hands, a shiver shook her shoulders. Did she believe him? Too late now. He might as well go for broke. Guarding his bruised ribs, he dug through his trouser pocket, extracted the box, and placed it in her palm.

"You showed me the way home to my family. But I'm nothing if you won't come with me, create a family and a home with me."

She didn't blink.

"Dana? I'm starting to worry."

Nothing. Kyle squeezed her hand. Her fingers felt cold and clammy. "Do you need more time?"

When she shook her head, a breath rushed from his lungs. But then, tears formed in her eyes.

"Please don't cry." He caught her tears with his thumbs. "You have the most amazing eyes. I could get lost in those eyes. Actually, I'd like to get lost in them for the rest of my life."

When she smiled, the pain along his ribs eased. "You can open it. Last I checked, there was nothing dangerous inside."

Her fingers brushed at the velvet sides three times before she popped it open with a snap. He thought it was the perfect ring for them, especially considering he'd found it at the last minute. Guilt caused a pinch in his neck, but he ignored it. After all, a little white lie about why he was late was allowed to purchase an engagement ring.

Kyle removed the ring and slid it on her finger. "The three

interwoven diamond bands are like a DNA strand. See?" He pointed at the row of sparkling chocolate brown diamonds. "This row represents me. The blue diamond strand is you. That was a challenge because your eye color seems to deepen with your mood. But blue diamonds are kind of rare, so I went for the darker color because your eyes were almost navy the first time I made love to you. They turn a similar shade when Sam hugs you. They're that same shade right now."

"Yes," she whispered.

Although he wasn't sure if she was agreeing to marry him or with the color assessment, he wasn't asking questions. "The brilliant clear diamonds are for Sam because she sparkles with innocence, energy, and enthusiasm. The three are entwined like our lives, our love."

When she straightened her arm, the diamonds reflected the tiny lights blinking on along the awnings of Main Street.

He kissed her fingertips. "I'm starting to worry here. I can take it back. You can pick out a ring you like better. Feedback would be appreciated about now."

Maybe he should let her sit down. She looked shocky. He hoped it was a good shock.

When her lips covered his, he almost lost his balance. Ryan would've been proud of the way he soldiered up and showed her with his kiss what his words failed to express. When he finally released her, he was hoping she'd be glassy-eyed. No dice. Color had returned to her cheeks.

"I hope that was code for yes."

She stiffened. "One caveat."

Uh-oh. The Dana he knew and loved had returned. "Anything you say, darling."

She wagged her finger at him. "'Darling'? Are you seriously calling me darling? Where the heck did that come from?"

He wrapped her arm in his and moved toward the hotel. "I have no idea. It just popped out on its own."

"I'm not sure I like it."

"The word will never pass these lips again." At this point, he'd play the biggest wussy in town if she'd say yes.

Her eyes had narrowed, but her lips twitched with a hint of a grin. "In the future, we make plans together. You can't purchase a clinic in a different town and just expect me to say, 'yes dear, anything you say.'"

"'Dear'?" Pain arced through his side, and he doubled at the waist, gasping for air.

"Kyle?" Her hands warmed his back. "Are you okay?"

"Just a few bumps and bruises," he choked out.

"I'm so sorry," Dana said. "Did they scan your body? You could have internal bleeding."

He should milk this for all it was worth, but the door to the hotel opened, and Sam stood in the entrance. From her desperate look, something had happened. Which he did not need. He was in enough trouble with Dana.

"Kyle, I need help," Sam said.

Dana hurried to her daughter faster than he could manage with his bum leg. "Are you okay?" Dana stooped in front of Sam. "Did something happen?"

Sam, her eyes moist with tears, looked over Dana's shoulder. "I didn't mean for him to get loose."

"Who?" Dana said.

Ignoring the spear in his side, Kyle bit back a groan and stooped beside his little girl—because she would be his daughter very soon. "No tears, sweetie. Whatever happened, I'll help you fix it, okay?"

"Bandit looked sad inside the cage. I just opened it a little crack."

Dana's fingers bit into his forearm despite her fake smile.

"Kyle, honey—" Oh boy, nothing like going from the pot to the fire. "What is a Bandit?"

From inside the hotel, someone screamed.

"They're scaring him," Sam wailed.

Kyle herded his soon-to-be family inside.

"There he goes," a male voice shouted.

"Eek!"

"It's under the table."

"I've got him, Samantha!" Noel crawled from under the table with the ferret Kyle had purchased for Sam cuddled in her arms. "I think he's scared."

Kyle's grandmother was sitting on the dining table. Talley was giggling. Nate stood, holding the open crate while Ava and Ryan Murphy laughed.

Sam hurried to Noel, her hands outstretched, but Kyle managed to beat her there. Bandit's heart was thumping as hard as his. In moments, he released the small ferret into the safety of the crate, and Nate closed the door.

"I think he's safer in his carrier for now, okay?" Kyle said.

"I don't want anything to happen to him." Sam stuck her fingers through the opening.

Dana crossed her arms over her chest. But before he could beg forgiveness, *again,* pain detonated in his side. He sidestepped a repeat of Whit's shoulder shove.

"Bro, you're on your own on this one. For a smart guy, you sure mess up a lot." He held out his hand to Sam. "Come on, girls. We'll take Bandit to our house. You can let him out on the screened porch and get to know him."

Talley patted Dana's shoulder. "Go easy on him. He's only got one good eye as it is."

While his family filed by and teased him about the situation, Dana stood and stared in silence. Whatever was going through that gorgeous head of hers was probably not going to be good for his case. Like he had a case.

Since the hotel staff had started stacking the dirty dishes in carts, he led her to the lobby and sat on the antique settee beside the empty fireplace. Good thing it was spring. She'd probably roast his sorry hide over the fire if it were winter.

"You bought Sam a ferret?"

He didn't think she'd appreciate being told the question was redundant and kept his mouth closed.

Her lip twitched again.

"I figured we could pay one of the cousins to ferret-sit while we're on our vacation."

Her brows shot toward her hairline. "*We're* going on vacation?"

"Vacation slash honeymoon."

He thought her brows had reached their maximum height. He'd been wrong.

"And where are *we* going?"

Man, she was starting to make him feel like a little kid. Then again, he'd kind of been acting like one for a while. Could be time to change.

Ignoring the multiple pains in his body, he grabbed her shoulders. "Dana Graham, I'm in love with you. I'm in love with the miniature you too. I want to make a family with you. I want you to be part of my family. I messed up today's ending, but it's fixable, just like I am. So quit giving me a hard time and kiss me."

Finally, she gave him the smile he'd been fantasizing about since he walked out of the ED.

"I thought you'd never ask."

DEAR READER,

I hope you enjoyed Murphy's Cinderella and will consider reading another book in my Clocktower Romance Series. Although the setting revolves around Sunberry, and the characters are friends or relatives, each book is a stand-alone novel and can be read in any order.

My romances contain zero to low heat levels. In the spicier romances, characters may use stronger language. Carolina Cowboy and Murphy's Secret are a little spicier, while Home to Stay, The Puppy Barter, Murphy's Cinderella, and my novella Loving Trouble are sweeter.

If you fell in love with the Murphy brothers and missed one of their stories, look for the boxed collection including Home to Stay, Murphy's Secret, and Murphy's Cinderella due to release in November.

PLEASE LEAVE A REVIEW

If you have enjoyed this book, please leave me a review on, Goodreads, Bookbub, and Amazon

Reviews help readers find books from people who have enjoyed a story and help me improve my craft. Yes, your opinion matters. If you can spare just five minutes to leave even a one or two line review, it would be so helpful in this book's success.

Thanks so much!

Becke

START AT KYLE'S BEGINNING!

Home to Stay

If you enjoyed Murphy's Cinderella, you will enjoy Home to the beginning of the Murphy legacy and check out teen Kyle, go to www.becketurner.com and select subscribe from the menu. Below is a sample.

———

HOME TO STAY EXCERPT

6:30 P.M.

Her boys couldn't be missing. Not today. Ava Robey checked the lane leading from Sunberry Road to the house. They weren't missing. They were late. And she had good news. They'd made it to the final round in the lease competition. If they won, Robey's Rewards would open in the only available commercial site on Main Street. One month of after-school and weekend work separated them from opening their new business.

But where were they? Her hand shook so hard she made

the cut too short. One six-inch piece of trim and the laminate floor she'd installed would be complete. Her eyes moistened.

Breathe. Don't panic. They'll be here.

Hope, her five-year-old daughter, stepped over the toolbox and stood with her chubby hands fisted on her hips. "Where are my boys? The barn light is on."

Ava shoved an errant tendril into the Marine bandana tied around her head. "They're with a new friend. They'll be here soon."

Careful to keep her trembling fingers away from the saw's edge, she cut another trim piece. Most days the wood scent, the smooth texture of the surface, and the dramatic transition of the project relaxed her. Not today. The pungent odor of the construction adhesive blasted through her sinuses like a lethal toxin.

Hope waited by her side until the scream of the saw died. "I don't like Kyle's friends."

"That's why we moved to Gran's farm," Ava answered, careful to hide the tension from her tone. "Kyle is making nice friends, now." She hoped.

Once she'd installed the final piece, Ava loaded her tools into Grandpa's hand-made box, wishing for his assurance that everything would work okay. So, what was keeping her three sons? They knew today was special.

6:35 P.M.

Ava straightened with a hand to her back, ignoring the aches brought on by hours on her hands and knees. Outside the front window, the leaves stirred along the desolate lane. She swallowed past a thickening in her throat. They're okay. Any minute, Kyle, Whit, and Nate would burst through the door with a hare-brained reason for their delay and hungry for dinner.

"We need to go get them," Hope demanded, her high

voice indicating near melt-down mode. "They're going to miss Daddy's memory party."

"No, munchkin." Ava bent on one achy knee. "They won't miss it. They'll be here soon. Why don't you throw the ball for Toby?"

The black lab sleeping near the pantry lifted his head and drummed his broad tail against the new wood floor.

Hope stomped a booted foot. "I want to eat!"

"I'll make dinner in a little while."

"Two minutes?" Hope held up two stubby fingers.

Breathe. It's not her fault the boys are late. "In ten minutes you can help me set the table for the party."

Hope brightened and raced to the throw pillow in front of the TV screen. "Jiffy is ready for my memory." She held up the battered stuffed pig. "See? I gave him a bath last night so he'd be pretty and clean."

"Good job."

Before her daughter noticed her tears, she picked up the toolbox and exited through the back door, the hinges creaking from her hasty retreat. Keeping her back to the doorway, Ava deposited the toolbox along the wall, pulled a wadded tissue from her pocket, and blotted her eyes. The last shards of daylight dropped behind the trees and darkened the orange and yellow leaves. Twilight blanketed the old farmhouse like depression had blanketed her life five years ago. She'd survived those dark years, like she'd survive her boys' teen years. Because after tonight, they'd be grounded until graduation!

"You need to call my boys and tell them to come home right now." Hope said, startling Ava with her proximity. "I see stars."

Ava shuddered. Why had she taken Kyle's cell phone? Because he'd left her no choice. And why hadn't she questioned him about the new friend when he'd called for permission? He had a new friend, and he'd called to ask. She'd been thrilled by his consideration. Two hours ago.

Keeping her head turned from the intense scrutiny of her daughter, she opened the cupboard door, and removed six plates. How did she fix this? She couldn't call the friend, couldn't drive to the house. She couldn't even call the police. What would she say? My boys are late for dinner? What if they'd been abducted?

Don't panic. They weren't little kids. All three had topped her five feet seven inches over a year ago. Sunberry, a small city located near the North Carolina coast, had its share of small-time crime. But who would pick up three boys? Not one lone child, who could be overcome and intimidated, but three good-sized adolescents who had seen the better side of far too many disagreements.

The dishes clattered in her trembling fingers. Had Kyle found trouble in Sunberry already? She'd hoped he would grow out of his rebellious streak, focus on his schoolwork. He was smart—and angry. Had he done something bad? Led his two younger brothers into trouble? A memory of Kyle's dark eyes once bright and loving faded into his current dark-edged gaze.

Hope tilted her head to the side. "Are you going to cry?"

Ava closed her eyes, inhaled, and then blew out a breath. "Not if I can get a hug from you."

Plump arms encircled her neck. She couldn't lose Hope or her boys. Ava hugged Hope close to her chest, careful to avoid squeezing too hard.

"Ooo," Hope cooed.

Heavens, she loved that funny sound, the tickle of her daughter's silky curls, and the scent of her strawberry shampoo. But her heart continued to race.

6:50 P.M.

Headlights illuminated the lane and Ava shifted for a

better view through the front window. Her heart pounded *lub-dub, lub-dub* in her ears. The boys had ridden their bikes to school this morning. A big black SUV bumped through the lane ruts, bouncing the beam of light across the living room wall. Thank goodness, it wasn't a police car. Although all traces of saliva abandoned her mouth, she swallowed past the constriction in her throat. *Never show weakness.*

The SUV stopped in the drive behind her aging Ford Explorer. When the headlights blinked out, the outlines of multiple passengers moved beneath the interior light. However, the tinted glass obscured the occupants' identities. The driver's door opened and a large man, dressed in desert fatigues, straightened in the dim light from the porch.

A memory sent a chill racing along her spine. The set of his wide shoulders seemed familiar. When he looked up, her heart skydived to the pit of her stomach and she slapped her palm over her mouth. No! Not now, after so long. Captain Murphy, a man she thought she'd never see again, moved toward the back of the SUV. Her three missing sons trailed behind him.

"Why you?" she whispered.

While Toby whined from his position at the front door, Captain Murphy helped lift the boys' bikes from the cargo area of the SUV.

Hope stepped beside her. "Are my boys with a stranger?"

Ava gripped the window ledge. How did she explain to her children the man in her driveway had given their father his final, fatal orders?

When she jerked on the doorknob, the door scraped against the threshold announcing yet another item on the repair list for Gran's old house. Now her sons had joined that list. Looking guilty as sin, they stood behind the Captain, their gazes fixed on the weathered porch boards.

From the other side of the screen, the Marine stared at her. "Ms. Robey."

Ava stepped back. "Come in. From the looks of the boys, your story will require time and a meal."

Fifteen-year-old Kyle shot her an uneasy glance but moved forward.

Whit, her second son, followed, his bright blues moist with unshed tears, a gash bisecting his right brow. "Sorry, Mom."

She reached to inspect his face. "Are you okay?"

He ducked out of her grasp. "It's nothing."

Ava lowered her hand. This wasn't the first time one of her boys had suffered a cut or had come home late. But they'd never done it on November third.

With the tattered pig clutched under her arm, Hope gave her three brothers a fierce look. "You made me wait for Memory Night. I'm not coloring any more pictures for you!"

"Shh, honey." Ava moved Hope aside to let them enter. "Let Mommy handle this, okay?"

"I've been waiting forever." Hope's pouty bottom lip trembled.

"Thank you for your patience. Now, go feed Toby so I can talk to this gentleman." Ava gave her sons a no-nonsense look to let them know they were in deep trouble. "We'll talk later. Clean up for dinner."

She met Kyle's angry brown eyes, so like his father's. For a moment, her resolve wobbled. Near the cusp of manhood, Kyle tested her authority at every opportunity. She squinted. Was his jaw swollen? When he glared back at her, she pointed toward the hallway. "Ten minutes and we're sitting down for dinner."

With her breath held, she waited. *Come on, Kyle. Don't display the family wrinkles in front of the Captain, even if we aren't military anymore.*

Fourteen-year-old Whit, the family peacemaker, wrapped one arm around Kyle and the other around twelve-year old Nate. Together, the boys started down the hall, two dark heads surrounding her fair-haired middle son. After two steps, Kyle looked over his shoulder, anger still glittering in his glance.

"He always has to get in the last word," she muttered.

"He's smart," Ryan spoke from behind her. "Men like Kyle make good Marines. *If* you can turn that anger into a constructive outlet."

She whirled to face him. "You can't have him. You can't have any of my sons."

Unlike Kyle, Ryan didn't break her gaze. Standing at well over six feet tall, he filled Gran's small entryway. Sorrow, not rage, however, glistened in his eyes. Compassionate eyes—the same as her second born.

Heat flashed up her neck and face. "Sorry, it's—" She motioned toward the adjacent kitchen. "Please, come in and sit down. Coffee?"

He pushed away from the doorjamb and followed her. "Don't go to any trouble on my account."

"You brought my sons home. Coffee is the least I can do." She placed two white mugs on the counter. "I hope decaf is okay. I avoid caffeine after noon."

She placed the coffee in front of him, noting the stiff set of his features. Ryan Murphy had a bigger than life presence, dwarfing her country-style kitchen. Even sitting at the long plank table built for a family of eight, his wide shoulders and long legs seemed too large for the bench her three sons usually occupied.

She glanced at him before removing the pitcher of batter from the refrigerator. "I've been laying new floor, so I mixed pancake batter before I started. Three growing boys are hard to fill. I always make a double recipe and have plenty."

He looked like he had a bad case of poison ivy and didn't know whether to scratch or suffer. At least that was her take. She'd never been able to read him. He'd been from a prominent Sunberry family. She'd grown up on the farm. Although her husband Josh had liked and respected Ryan, she'd only been around him in later years at functions like the Marine Corps Ball.

While he sipped coffee behind her, she prepped the grill and poured syrup in a saucepan to warm. After ten years as a military wife, the rules remained stamped in her brain. Josh was enlisted. Ryan was an officer. She'd never seen Captain Murphy attempt to link the gap. In all fairness, the military wives often bridged the ranks and Ryan was single. At least he used to be.

When she sat at the table, he straightened. "So, you installed the floor by yourself?"

"The boys help me on the weekends. I finished the living room about ten minutes before you arrived." A burst of pride flamed in her chest. She'd done a good job once she'd figured out how to cut the corners.

"A woman with tools? I'm impressed. My sisters might have hung a few posters if I wasn't available." He smiled, and his features underwent a startling transition.

Her hand drifted to her chest. Amazing how a simple expression changed a man's looks.

She shrugged to hide her unexpected reaction. Must be the dimple on the right side of his mouth.

"Gran's house is rough. No one's lived here in years. When Mom and I opened the door that first day, we almost hightailed it back to Charlotte."

"Sorry to hear about your mother."

Her breath hitched. Despite the leaking roof, deteriorating floors, and molding walls, she and Mom hadn't given up, hadn't given in to weakness. They'd laughed so hard they'd cried. Ava blinked. They'd had a good run. She wiped the tear at the corner of her eye and sipped her coffee, letting the warm liquid soothe her the same way Mom once had.

She blew out a breath. "So, what's the story on my boys?"

The man wasn't model material. His nose had a bump in the middle and his chin-line bore sporadic pock marks from teen acne. Still, he had a confident look—like a man who knew and understood himself and his world. A jab of resentment poked at the back of her mind. He hadn't known too much about Afghanistan. Otherwise Josh would still be alive.

"They were in a fight. I broke it up. Afterward, I made a deal with them. Based on your approval, of course."

The thought of being obligated to the man caused her fingers to curl around her mug. "Captain Murphy."

"Major now, but please, call me Ryan."

"Ryan." His name rolled off her tongue smooth as hot syrup on cakes. "Thanks for bringing my boys home. There's light traffic on our road, but I don't like them riding their bikes on it after dark."

He held up his palm. "I'd like to give your boys time to tell their side of the story before we talk. There's nothing worse than having a grown-up rat you out before you get a chance to come clean." He paused, opened and closed large calloused hands. "I mean if it's okay with you." He dipped his chin. "Sorry. I'm used to making decisions."

Big surprise, there. Still, she liked the idea. Not because it was his. Truth be known, she wanted *not* to like it.

"If there are any..." He held her gaze. "Holes in their account, I'll bring you up to speed afterwards. Since I'm involved, I've also got an idea about consequences—at least how I want to be repaid."

Repaid? Okay, she *really* didn't like that, especially when they were close to acquiring their dream. What the dickens had her boys gotten into? She sipped the decaf and released a slow breath. The time she'd charged into the principal's office to find her boys had told her *part* of the story flashed in her mind.

"Fair enough." She stood. "Boys! Five-minute warning."

When she topped off his cup, the steam swirled upward. "Family dinner time is important. That's when we talk. How many cakes do you eat?"

He pushed to his feet. "I'll come back after dinner."

"Don't." Blood pounded in her ears. "Dinner is my way of thanking you for bringing them home. Don't take that away from me."

His gaze sparked with an emotion she couldn't read. "Three big ones or six small ones."

When she removed the griddle from the pan drawer, the metal clanked grating against her already frayed nerves. Darn her boys for putting her in this situation. She wanted them to like Sunberry, make friends, be normal. Heat flushed her cheeks. This better not be the new Robey normal.

Major Murphy remained ramrod straight, his sleeves rolled up his forearms, but his gaze flicked around the area. Josh used to do that. He never missed a thing. She sprayed the marred surface of the grill to keep the pancakes from sticking. Everything about the scene was flawed—like Gran's rundown place, her holey jeans, faded Marine t-shirt, and her hair tied beneath one of Josh's old handkerchiefs. At least the new floor looked good.

The gas burner on her range sputtered and then flickered to life along with something long buried within her—awareness of a man. Her scalp tingled, and guilt churned her stomach. She'd buried Josh five years ago and not one time had she thought of a man—any man. Right, like a widow with four children and a sick mother had time to think about a social life. Heck, she hadn't even seen an eligible man in the last year—unless she counted Bennie, the handy man she used for jobs exceeding her skills.

"Mom and I moved back to Sunberry because Kyle kept making the wrong kind of friends in Charlotte."

The batter hit the griddle with a sizzle, breaking the silence.

"Whit tries to talk Kyle out of getting in trouble. Nate doesn't challenge anyone. He follows his big brother." Stop babbling. The man didn't need to know about her family problems. But one thing he *did* need to know.

She turned to gauge his reaction. "Tonight is Memory Night."

Silence. Within seconds he stiffened with a slide of his boots and a widening of his eyes. Her breath hissed through her teeth. He knew the significance of the date.

"Every November third, we share a memory to remember and honor Josh." Her voice, rusty at the start, sounded stronger. "We'll all share a memory about Josh. You'll go last. I'm sure you can come up with something to tell them about their father. After that, the boys will explain why they were late."

When he started to push to his feet, her blood heated.

"Josh was a good man." She glared at Ryan. "You owe his sons at least one story about their dad.

Get your free eBook at your favorite retailer.

PLEASE STAY IN TOUCH!

Thank you for the opportunity to share Kyle Murphy's journey for love and his return to my Sunberry world. I hope you liked Kyle and Dana's love story. If so, you might be interested in Murphy's Secret, Whit and Talley's romance, and Home to Stay, which features the teen Murphy boys.

If you enjoyed your visit to Sunberry and would like to know more about my CLOCKTOWER ROMANCES, you can connect with me in the following ways:

1. Leave me a review and follow me on Amazon and Goodreads.
2. Follow me on Bookbub and Amazon.
3. Refer me to a friend.
4. Become a Book Mate and SIGN up for my TURNER TOWN Newsletter from my website. All subscribers are sent links to Becke's Book Mates, my private FB group.
5. Like my Facebook fan page, BECKE TURNER AUTHOR
6. Visit my website: www.Becketurner.com

7. Read my health tips blog on my website.

I love to hear from readers. If you subscribe, you will receive the following items:

- Monthly newsletter, Turner Town News, updates
- Book Mates, my private Facebook group, invitation
- Stories behind the stories that I only provide to subscribers
- Video clips
- Book sale alerts
- Cover reveals
- New releases
- Health tips
- Recipes
- More free stuff

If you subscribe, I will never share your information. I value your time and appreciate your interest in my work. If you find in the future you no longer want book notifications and free items, you may unsubscribe at any time. To join, go to www.becketurner.com and fill out the subscribe form.

Thank you for your support of my books. As a special thank you, I've added the recipe for Chewy Hazelnut-Browned Butter Sugar Cookies to sweeten your day.

Thanks again for reading.

BOOKS BY BECKE TURNER

In a Clocktower Romance the setting and the characters are friends or relatives, but each book is a stand-alone novel and can be read in any order.

My romances are rated PG-13. In 2022 I revised Carolina Cowboy and Murphy's Secret to align with my Sweet Romance Brand for the CLOCKTOWER ROMANCE Series. However, I included a link to the omitted bedroom scene to allow my readers to choose. The characters and the plot remain the same.

I hope this explanation helps you with your next selection. Enjoy!

————

HOME TO STAY (Award-Winning Murphy Clan Beginning)

CAROLINA COWBOY

- *LOVING TROUBLE (companion novella to CAROLINA COWBOY)*

MURPHY'S SECRET (Whit Murphy's romance)

THE PUPPY BARTER

MURPHY'S CINDERELLA (Kyle Murphy's romance)

MURPHY'S CHOICE (Nate Murphy's romance)

A SUNBERRY CHRISTMAS (December 9, 2022 release)

————

Want a bigger bang for your buck? Choose a 3-book collection!

THE CLOCKTOWER ROMANCE COLLECTION

- *HOME TO STAY*
- *CAROLINA COWBOY*
- *MURPHY'S SECRET*

THE MURPHY MEN COLLECTION

- *HOME TO STAY*
- *MURPHY'S SECRET*
- *MURPHY'S CINDERELLA*

THE FEEL GOOD COLLECTION

- *HOME TO STAY*
- *THE PUPPY BARTER*
- *MURPHY'S CINDERELLA*

CHEWY HAZELNUT-BROWNED BUTTER SUGAR COOKIES

Makes 24 cookies
Ingredients

- 2¼ cups (11¼ ounces) all-purpose flour
- 1 teaspoon baking powder
- ½ teaspoon baking soda
- ½ teaspoon table salt
- 1½ cups (10½ ounces) sugar, plus ⅓ cup for rolling, divided
- 2 ounces cream cheese, cut into 8 pieces
- ¼ cup finely chopped toasted skinned hazelnuts. Substituted butterscotch chips
- 6 tablespoons unsalted butter
- ⅓ cup vegetable oil
- 1 large egg
- 2 tablespoons whole milk

Directions

1. Adjust oven rack to middle position and heat oven to 350 degrees. Line 2 baking sheets with parchment paper.

Whisk flour, baking powder, baking soda, and salt together in bowl.

2. Place 1½ cups sugar, cream cheese, and hazelnuts in large bowl. Melt butter in 10-inch skillet over medium-high heat, then continue to cook, swirling skillet constantly, until butter is dark golden brown and has nutty aroma, 1 to 3 minutes. Immediately whisk browned butter into sugar and cream cheese (some lumps of cream cheese will remain). Whisk in oil until incorporated. Whisk in egg and milk until smooth. Using rubber spatula, fold in flour mixture until soft, homogeneous dough forms.

3. Spread remaining ⅓ cup sugar in shallow dish. Working with 2 tablespoons dough at a time, roll into balls, then roll in sugar to coat; space dough balls 2 inches apart on prepared sheets. Using bottom of greased dry measuring cup, press each ball until 3 inches in diameter. Using sugar left in dish, sprinkle 2 teaspoons sugar over each sheet of cookies; discard extra sugar. (Raw cookies can be frozen for up to 1 month.)

4. Bake cookies, 1 sheet at a time, until edges are set and beginning to brown, 11 to 13 minutes (17 to 22 minutes if baking from frozen), rotating sheet halfway through baking. Let cookies cool on sheet for 5 minutes, then transfer to wire rack. Let cookies cool completely before serving.

Murphy's Cinderella

Written by Becke Turner

Cover Design by Ebook Cover Designs

Edited by JJ Kirkmon

Published by Special-T Publishing, LLC

ISBN - 978-1-953651-12-9

Library of Congress Control Number:

First Edition

First Printing --

Webpage: https://www.becketurner.com

Facebook: https://www.facebook.com/rebecca.turner.5891

Twitter: https://twitter.com/BeckeTurner

Amazon Author Page: https://www.amazon.com/Becke-Turner/e/B08N9RDR19

FB Author: https://www.facebook.com/Becke-Turner-Author-113219977250594

Goodreads Author Page: Goodreads.com/user/show/15034744

Book Mates: www.becketurner.com/?page_id=1076

Newsletter: TURNER TOWN

Health Blog: https://becketurner.com/category/blog

Made in the USA
Columbia, SC
25 September 2024

42382783R00135